SECRETS ON THE COTE D'AZUR

MYDWORTH MYSTERIES #8

Neil Richards • Matthew Costello

D1615821

RED DOG
UK

Published by RED DOG PRESS 2021

Copyright © Matthew Costello and Neil Richards 2021

Matthew Costello and Neil Richards have asserted their right under the Copyright, Designs and Patents Act, 1988 to be identified as the authors of this work
This book is sold subject to the condition that it shall not by way of trade or otherwise, be lent, resold, hired out, or otherwise circulated without the publisher's prior consent in any form of binding or cover other than that in which it is published and without a similar condition including this condition being imposed on the subsequent purchaser

Originally published as an eBook edition by Bastei Lübbe AG, Cologne, Germany, 2021.

Edited by Eleanor Abraham
Cover Design by Oliver Smyth

ISBN 978-1-913331-17-7

www.reddogpress.co.uk

1.

A SUNSET TO REMEMBER

PERCY PORTER CLIMBED down onto the dusty platform of Cannes train station and stepped away from the hurrying crowds. He watched as station staff, busy with their flags and whistles, readied the train for its departure.

He tilted his white panama hat against the last of the evening sun, then leaned on his Malacca cane, hand firm on the silver grip.

Motionless, he took in every last detail of this wondrous evening: the distant snow-capped Alps; the black and white smoke billowing from the engine; the chattering crowds; the cooking aromas, wafting up from the town, mixing with the snatches of cigar smoke; the reddening sky to the west, and the rich blue above.

What bliss, he thought.

Then, as the train pulled away, steam puffing, wheels screeching, he turned and headed down into the maze of streets that led to the sea, the Croisette and his hotel.

WHY DID I never realise that life could be like this? he thought, as he ambled through the bustling streets, the warm evening air rich with smells, sights and sounds.

Why, in my fifty years on this earth, have I never known what it is to feel truly happy… till now?

Of course, he knew the answer to *that* question.

One word – and he smiled as he said it softly to himself.

"Simone."

He realised that his whole existence could be defined as life *before* Simone and now… *life with* Simone.

Before she'd entered his world, his days in England had been all grey cloudy skies, damp cobbled streets, and bitter winds. Noisy factories, bottling plants, smoke-filled boardrooms, bankers' drafts, industrial disputes.

Endless tins of tomato soup, egg-and-cress sandwiches, countless mugs of stewed tea.

More like a prison than a life.

And after his day of work? His evenings and weekends had been spent in silent suppers with his wife Alice in the gloomy drawing room of Nantwich Hall, the monotony broken only by occasional dull dinners with half the mayors of the north-west of England and their grim spouses; or polite afternoon teas with bland vicars, dim-witted aristocrats; and visits from Alice's snooty in-laws from the Home Counties, always moaning, criticising, complaining about something… anything.

What a fool he had been to live *that* life, when *this* life was so readily available to be lived.

Life with Simone.

A joyous and dreamlike existence in which the weather was so unbelievably pleasant, the food so much tastier, the colours brighter, the people charming, and every day was an impossibly fresh, new adventure. The beautiful Mediterranean always – quite simply – *stunning*.

He strolled now – past familiar cafés and shops –

recognising waiters and regulars, exchanging cheery *"bonsoirs"* and *"monsieurs"*. Finally, he reached the Croisette, the long tree-lined avenue that ran the length of the curved Cannes bay. He paused, tipped his hat, and smiled at a well-dressed young couple – their arms entwined, laughing – as if recognising like-souls, also under the spell of this wondrous place.

The couple smiled back – and he knew that they were in love and he guessed that they could, through some lovers' instinct, see that he, *too*, was truly, madly in love.

In love with Simone.

Just the thought of her... dizzying!

In love with her brown eyes, her knowing smile, her beautiful soft skin, her boundless energy, her crazy ideas, her serious thoughts, her gentle soul, her sinuous dancing, sublime singing, and – always – *those brown eyes, gazing into his.*

He looked down now along the Croisette, positively *filled* with elegant couples promenading before dinner. White horse-drawn coaches passed back and forth, the clomping of hooves sounding rhythmic with nearby palm trees swaying gently.

The sea had now turned a luminous green, and to the west, over the Esterel Mountains, the setting sun made the red earth there seem to blaze with colour, as if alive.

He looked east, down the Croisette, past his own hotel, the Carlton. If the Pointe Croisette and the harbour weren't in the way, he fancied he just might be able to see all the way down the coast to lovely Antibes, where, even now, Simone was surely lying on her silk-draped bed, sleeping gently, resting before dinner.

He smiled to himself, remembering that sweetly scented apartment from just an hour ago, that afternoon-warm bed.

Then, alarmingly – for a second – a harsh voice, unbidden.

For a moment he thought it was the brittle tones of his wife Alice –her sharp voice a dagger in his heart.

He spun round, fearful that she might actually be there – but placed his hand against his chest in relief as he saw a bickering English couple march past, the husband staring miserably at the pavement, the line of children behind them, straight-backed, on best behaviour.

He laughed to himself again. How could it possibly be Alice? Alice wasn't due to come to the Riviera for another month.

No need to fear her appearance yet!

Yes. Plenty of time to work out an amicable solution to this miraculous about-turn his life appeared to have taken.

Hmm, I must take some time to figure out how to handle that, he thought.

But, feeling relieved that *that* moment hadn't yet come, he again looked down the promenade at the long line of elegant, white-stuccoed hotels.

Time for a sundowner, he thought.

And where better than the rooftop bar on that smart new hotel, the Martinez!

Yes, it was pricey. Extremely pricey! But, as Percy now knew (because darling Simone kept telling him), *"Money is there to be spent – to be enjoyed, mon cheri!"*

Off he strolled towards the dramatic Martinez Hotel, facing the now-darkening Med, wondering which of their new-fangled cocktails he should try this evening, and already contemplating whether to have the salt-baked bass or the lobster for dinner.

THREE HOURS LATER, and feeling rather tipsy – *though who cares?* – he spun through the revolving doors of his hotel, the Carlton (*twice round, once more for fun!*) and crossed the empty marble-floored vestibule to reception.

"Monsieur Porter, *bonsoir*," said the night receptionist.

"*Mon cher Gaston*, my old friend, my rock of ages," said Percy stepping forward and leaning unsteadily against the reception, panama under one arm.

He beamed for a few seconds at the young man in the perfect suit, his lapel badge shining. "Wasn't it a beautiful sunset?"

"I'm sure it was, sir," said Gaston. "I hope sir has passed a pleasant day?"

"Oh, much *more* than pleasant," said Percy. He stepped back and did a full twirl. A *pirouette* – just like the one he had done this morning for Simone on the beach in Antibes. "My entire day was… *delightful!* Delicious! Superb! In fact, all of the above!"

"I am very happy for you, sir," said Gaston, and Percy saw him smile.

Always fun to try to get these young fellas to come out of their shells, he thought.

"Your key, sir?"

"Key?" said Percy. "But, Gaston, the night is yet young!"

Then he realised his head *was* beginning to swim a little (*that last cognac, perhaps? A bit trop?*) The thought of his bed growing more attractive by the second.

He swayed slightly as Gaston handed him his room key, on a giant tassel bigger than the ones on the curtains at Nantwich Hall.

"Oh! I nearly forgot," said Gaston. "There is mail for you,

sir."

Percy frowned as he saw the receptionist retrieve a large brown envelope from the pigeonholes behind him, and hand it over.

He inspected the cover.

"To Monsieur P Porter. Personal and Confidential. Addressee only."

Strange, he thought. *I'm not expecting anything at all. Office would have telephoned, surely, if any contracts needed signing?*

"Er, did you see who left it for me?" he said.

"Non, monsieur," said Gaston. "I was not yet on duty."

Percy turned the envelope over in his hands. Suddenly some instinct told him not to open it here. He tucked it under his arm.

"Well, life is full of surprises, my boy, don't you find?" said Percy.

"It is indeed, sir."

"Well, a very *bonne nuit* to you!"

"*À vous aussi,*" said Gaston.

And Percy headed for the elevator, already looking forward to the daily challenge of the intricate Art Deco doors.

PERCY ENTERED HIS room, turned on the lights and threw his hat, cane, key and package on the bed.

The doors out to his balcony were already open, the gentle evening breeze making the curtains sway.

He stepped out and took in the brilliantly beautiful view of Cannes, still lit up, a moon now rising over the deep, black sea.

Then he turned back into the room and picked up the large envelope.

What on earth could it be? Ah – a present from Simone perhaps!

The flap was gummed down and also taped closed. *Very secure!* He pulled clumsily at the tape and finally got the thing open. Inside he quickly could see what looked like… photographs, and a single folded sheet of paper.

He pulled out the paper, opened it, to reveal…

Not a present from Simone.

A message formed from cut-up letters and words from newspapers or magazines. He read the simple message, the words piercing his soul like arrows: TWENTY THOUSAND FRANCS TOMORROW OR THESE GO PUBLIC.

These? he thought, suddenly alarmed. *What the hell…?*

He hurriedly reached into the packet, tearing, scrabbling at the envelope, until it *sprung open* and half a dozen photographs scattered onto the bed.

He stepped back in horror.

The photographs – *of him and Simone* – he recognised instantly, from this last joyous week with her in Antibes.

Intimate photographs. Their sweet moments of *love*, turned into… *obscenity!*

Flinging an arm in front of his eyes, as if he might be able to pretend the photos didn't exist, he staggered back from the bed until he hit the wall with a thud. Shaking now, not from alcohol but from this horrible *threat.*

He sank to the floor, sobbing, praying for the world to swallow him up.

All of this day's happiness now terribly twisted… into anger, pain, loss… despair.

He listened to his own sobbing – chest heaving – as if the sound came from someone else, someone who sounded doomed.

And he had the terrible thought: *That person is me.*

2.

STRANGERS ON A TRAIN

KAT REILLY – these days more widely known in England as Lady Katherine Mortimer – watched as her husband Harry eased the cork from a bottle of champagne, the cork escaping with a satisfying hiss.

"*Parfait!*" he said, pouring the bubbly into two crystal flutes and handing one to her.

To make things even more perfect, she heard the massive steam locomotive vent a loud whistle, then felt the carriages jolt as the famous, incredibly luxurious, "Train Bleu" eased out of the Gare de Lyon – destination: the French Riviera.

For a girl from the Bronx... quite a moment.

"Oops!" said Harry, steadying himself on the wall of the sleeper compartment. Then he raised his glass to hers and *clinked*.

"*À votre santé!*" said Kat, taking a sip and sitting on the cushioned bench. "Mmm, delicious."

"Pommery. Only the absolute best for the first drink of the holiday, don't you think? Or should that be – *vacation*?"

"It doesn't become a 'vacation' until after you've wrapped up your meetings in Nice," said Kat. "Until then, I'm trying to think of it as just a 'work trip'."

"Wise words!" said Harry. "Though, I must say, not many

work trips include a couple of top-of-the-range sleeping compartments, private bathrooms and first-class dining – and that's just for starters! I do think the actual Riviera will be right up your alley."

"And – look – even a glimpse of the Eiffel Tower," said Kat, nodding to the window as Paris slid by in the early evening light. "By the way, do we dress for dinner?"

"Oh, my dear, but of course. Part of the fun! And I have it on good authority that the Wagons Lit Company not only offers the finest gourmet dining, but also a rather extensive wine list."

"Shame they don't stretch to double beds," said Kat, eyes glowing, glancing around at the single compartment, and giving Harry a familiar smile.

"Oh, I know. Surprisingly un-French in that respect, eh? However, never fear, I shall keep the door open between the compartments and whisper sweet nothings to you all night long until you are fast asleep."

Kat, champagne flute in hand, took a step closer to her husband.

"Oh, I expect way more than that," said Kat. *This train was fun, but then, so was her husband.* "Meanwhile, more champagne please, it's delicious."

"*Mais bien sûr, madame,*" said Harry, pouring a top-up, then Kat saw him disappear into his own compartment for a second – and return with a bowl of olives.

"Rule one of French sleeper trains – tip the carriage attendant the minute you arrive, and you'll be looked after like a king. Or should that be emperor?"

"Whichever," said Kat, taking an olive and raising her glass. "*Vive la France!*"

"*Vive la revolution* too, just to be on the safe side," said Harry, helping himself to olives and joining her on the seat, as the suburbs of Paris drifted by in the soft evening light.

HARRY SAT BACK in the elegant dining car, while the waiter carved the most elegant slices of tender roast lamb, and served steaming vegetables from silver bowls.

"*Madame, monsieur*," he said, bowing slightly and withdrawing.

Harry took a sip of red wine.

Perfect! A Chateau Margaux 1920, a wine he adored, and the vintage he preferred. Ever more rare and pricey. But on this train? Not an issue.

"*Bon appétit*," he said, raising his glass to Kat's, and they began to eat.

Kat looked a million dollars in a deep-blue low-cut shimmering silk dress, the diamond necklace he had given her on their anniversary sparkling in the lantern-lit dining car.

He knew she wasn't one for much jewellery, but when she wore an item, *she wore it well.*

Outside was darkness – broken only by the occasional moodily lit station as they swept through the night southwards.

The dining car had quickly filled, but he had reserved – aided by more francs changing hands – a cosy table for two at one end, just perfect for watching the crowd, and barely in earshot of the other tables.

Just how Harry always liked it when on *business*. And, in truth, this was indeed a "business" trip.

His work on an occasional basis for a small and discrete branch of British Intelligence was not terribly demanding. But this trip was important. He had been tasked with debriefing an agent returning from North Africa after a long year undercover.

The "office", however, had had no objection to his taking Kat with him and bolting a week's holiday onto the expedition.

"So then, when do you meet your contact?" said Kat, as if reading his mind.

"*Right.* Tomorrow morning, I hope, if we arrive on time," said Harry. "Was aiming to get it out of the way, so we can quickly move onto enjoying ourselves for the rest of the week."

"Like your thinking, Sir Harry. You know the man? What's his name… Groves?"

"Wyndham Groves, that's right. Not really. Bumped into him a couple of times in Whitehall. Quite the old hand, I heard, and, word is, a good sort. Oodles of experience."

"You can share details, I hope. Despite it being hush-hush and all that."

"Oh, don't you worry – I will," said Harry, smiling.

When he and Kat had first met in Cairo at a US embassy reception, he had soon realised that, like him, her "diplomatic" title had been cover for a rather more *secret* role serving her country.

"Ah well, while you have all the fun playing the *ancient game*, I shall do a little shopping, pick up some summer frocks. Can't let you down by wearing last year's colours."

"You? Let me down? Never happen," said Harry. "Was thinking, perhaps, when I'm done, we'd hit *la plage* late afternoon? Then cocktails and dinner somewhere, *à deux*?"

"Sounds perfect," said Kat, reaching out and placing her hand on his on the starched white table cloth. "Though we mustn't forget Aunt Lavinia, of course."

Harry laughed. His aunt had been staying in Antibes for a few weeks, and the moment she had heard they were coming

SECRETS ON THE COTE D'AZUR

to Nice she was determined to make sure they were invited to all the right parties.

"Lavinia? Doubt she'll let that happen, I can assure you. By the end of the week we'll want to go into hiding, I'm sure."

He saw Kat smile, then noticed she was staring at something over his shoulder. Rather than turn, he said: "Seen something?"

"That obvious?" she said. "I must be out of practice."

"Oh, I don't think anyone else would have noticed. I'm a very attentive chap, least when it comes to you. What is it?"

"Okay. Take a look in the mirror behind me. There's a man sitting two tables down, on his own…"

Harry glanced nonchalantly at the ornate mirror above her head, which gave a view of the whole carriage behind him.

All the tables were fully occupied but, at one, an elderly man in a white suit sat alone. Moustache, wavy white hair, a single eye-glass.

"Yes, I see him," he said, casually taking another mouthful of the delicious meal. "Something up?"

"Hard to tell at this distance," said Kat. "But I'd wager *that* is no old man."

"Oh really? And the tell?"

"Hair's good. Moustache too. Tired old suit, very appropriate. But the hands – I can see from here – are the hands of a young man."

Harry checked the mirror again.

"Ah, yes. You're *right*. How very interesting."

Harry's first thought was: *Is he here for me? Am I being followed? Watched?* He did have ghosts from the past who would be very interested in whatever he was up to.

But it seemed unlikely. Easier just to pick up his trail at Nice station if some foreign power was genuinely interested in his little trip to the Riviera.

"Rather a beginner's error," said Kat, putting down her knife and fork and taking a sip of the Margaux.

"Which makes one ask the question," said Harry, "spy, thief, conman…?"

"Well, now that we are onto him, doubtless we shall find out before our little trip is over."

"*Indeed*," said Harry. "Intriguing. I do hope he stays for dessert. Cheese and port would be in character, for sure. I'd hate to miss any fireworks."

"Me too," she said.

He grinned at Kat, and she smiled back, dinner suddenly – with this discovery – *exciting*.

TWO HOURS LATER, and the dining car had all but emptied. Harry nodded goodnight to a young couple as they passed on the way back to the sleeping cars. Leaving just the mysterious old man – and Harry and Kat.

"How very interesting," said Harry. "I do believe *we* might be the mark."

"It's possible. Either way, well, this is good fun."

Harry beckoned to the waiter, and, when the bill came, he paid it ostentatiously with cash from his wallet. He saw in the mirror above Kat's head that the old man was watching the transaction.

"How shall we play it?" said Kat, quietly, when the waiter had left.

"Oh, a well-disguised chap like that? Imagine he'll make the first move."

And, sure enough, barely a minute later, the man in the

white suit paid his bill also, rose from his table, as if it was an effort, and, eyes straight ahead, trudged past them on his way to the sleeping cars.

Harry gave him a couple of minutes' head start, then, with a nod to Kat, got up and followed.

He opened the glass door to the first of the sleeping cars, and walked slowly down the narrow aisle, the train swaying as it hurtled through the night. But he didn't have to go far before he saw... a wallet lying on the floor.

Ah, he thought. *That scam.*

Smiling to himself, he picked it up and opened it, playing the part of the suddenly surprised traveller. Inside, a business card, the name *Henri Jacques, Insurance Agent* embossed in gold.

He knew he wouldn't have to wait long. Sure enough, the old man appeared from the next car, and seeing Harry with the wallet, shuffled at some speed, as if agitated, down the corridor towards him.

"Ah, monsieur! *Merci à Dieu!* You 'ave found it! My – how you say – wal-let?"

"Ah, yes. You must have dropped it, old boy," said Harry, handing it to him. "Monsieur Jacques?"

"*Oui, c'est moi!*" said the man, taking the wallet. "I cannot thank you enough!"

"Any time, monsieur. Happy to be of service."

Harry heard the door to the dining car open behind him, and knew that it would be Kat.

"Everything all right, darling?" she said, joining him, ready to play her part.

"Oh fine, my angel," said Harry, enjoying his husbandly role. "You go on ahead, I'll be with you in a minute."

He watched her as she squeezed past the two of them – the

old man attempting a formal bow in the uncomfortably tight space – and carried on to the end of the car.

There – instead of going through into the next car – he saw her turn and wait, arms folded. The perfect spot to enjoy the little scenario playing out down the corridor.

Harry now watched the old man pause before putting the wallet away – then open it, and rifle through the note sections, before looking up, alarmed…

"Monsieur," he said, eyes wide. "Non! There must be some mistake. I had nearly ten thousand francs in here. It is gone! *Disparu!*"

"Oh really?" said Harry. "Ten thousand, you say? Are you absolutely sure it was in there?"

"But of course! And the waiter – he will vouch for it, he saw the notes himself when I paid my bill."

"Now, that is peculiar. But I wonder… where *could* all those francs have gone?"

"Where indeed, monsieur!" said the old man, doing his best to seem both elderly and agitated. And Harry picked up the sudden hint of accusation in his voice.

"Oh! Surely you are not suggesting that I…" said Harry.

"But you 'ave found the wallet! Was in *your* hands! The francs are gone! This is robbery! In bold daylight, on the Train Bleu!"

Harry discounted the fact that outside it was actually the middle of the night and tried not to smile as he noticed Kat approaching silently from the end of the corridor.

"So, let's be clear here, um, Monsieur Jacques," he said. "Are you accusing me of taking your money?"

"I am! And I shall summon the guard to check your wallet *immédiatement!*"

SECRETS ON THE COTE D'AZUR

"You're sure you haven't just misplaced your cash?" said Harry, seeing Kat just a yard behind the old man, still unnoticed. "Perhaps, put it in your pocket?"

"Of course not!" said the man, his voice now raised. "What do you take me for? A gentleman would never stuff money in a *pocket*!"

"Oh, *really*?" said Kat. And Harry saw her quickly dip her hand into the old man's jacket pocket and pull out a wad of notes. "Well, I wonder what these could be?"

"What?" said the old man, spinning round (*rather too athletically*, Harry thought).

"*Mon Dieu*. Perhaps this is the missing cash?" said Kat, looking so innocent.

The old man stopped dead, patting his jacket pocket to check, then clearly revising his strategy. Harry thought of the phrase used by gamblers when stuck with a bad hand: *twist or bust.*

"*Zut alors!*" said the man. "Yes it is! Madame – *merci beaucoup!* I have clearly made the most dreadful, foolish mistake."

For effect, the man slapped his forehead as if age had led to his confusion over the misplaced francs.

Harry watched as Kat now unfolded the notes and spread the wad like a pack of cards. He could see that though the top and bottom note were indeed genuine 100-franc notes, the middle of the stack was just plain, cut paper.

"Ah," said the old man, doing a good job of looking dumbfounded, any logical explanation having gone completely out the window. "Um, surely this is some *erreur…*"

"Only mistake you made, pal," said Kat, "was to pick us two as stooges."

Harry saw her reach across and rip the old man's moustache

from his face in one brutally swift move.

"Ouch," said the old man in an American accent. "Hey, that hurt, dammit!"

At which point, she lifted his hat and plucked his white wig from his head.

To reveal – as Kat had intuited – a much younger man, barely in his twenties, Harry thought. Dark hair, and a make-up line where the wig had been.

"Well, well," said Harry. "Looks like the game's up *Henri Jacques*."

"Ha, guess so," said the man, with a shrug, forcing a grin as if this was all a jolly game, then leaning back casually against the carriage window. "Tell me – how'd you nail me?"

"The hands," said Kat.

"Oh dammit. Ran right out of the *slap* I normally use, you see," said the young man. "Thought I'd get away with it." His grin widened. "Seems not."

Kat nodded. "The acting was good – give you that. And the French accent."

"Hey, you're American too? Fancy that! You think maybe a bit over the top on the *zut alors*, huh?"

Harry laughed. "Maybe."

"But the wallet scam? Really?" said Kat. "Schoolboy stuff."

"Yeah, I know," said the man, with a wide-open grin. "But heck, it works most often enough times to pay for a hotel for the night, even a good dinner. No one wants a scandal on le Train Bleu!"

"What's your real name?" said Harry, more amused than angry.

"Roscoe," he said cheerily, holding out his hand for them to shake. "Roscoe Burns."

"New Yorker too, huh?" said Kat. "Fact… Bronx, if I'm not mistaken."

"Hey. You got it – takes one to know one," said Roscoe, smiling. "Grew up right on the Grand Concourse. Been a while."

Then he looked from Kat to Harry, those eyes suddenly looking serious, concerned.

"So what are you two gonna do? Call the guard? Have me arrested when we stop to take on water?"

Harry looked at Kat. Somehow he couldn't bear to send the kid to jail. Such a petty scam, anyway. Plus, last thing Harry needed was to get tied up as a witness in the morning.

He saw Kat shrug, and guessed she knew what he was thinking.

"You know what, Roscoe?" said Kat. "The night is still young. So why don't we buy you a nightcap in the bar and you can tell us how a nice kid from the Bronx ended up pulling lousy scams on the Train Bleu for a living?"

Together they turned and headed for the bar.

As they walked, Roscoe said, "But, you see, not all my scams are lousy." His grin wide again. "Tell you all about them."

"Oh, we're all ears," said Harry, smiling at Kat.

"Eyes too," she said, as Roscoe pushed open the door into the crowded, late-night bar. "Case you get any clever ideas about pulling another one."

3.

THE CÔTE D'AZUR!

KAT FLUNG OPEN the double windows of their bedroom at the Hotel Negresco and breathed in a delicious waft of salty sea air, all mixed with the scents of mimosas and hibiscus.

She stepped out onto the tiny Juliet balcony of the *ridiculously* expensive suite, and took in the panorama of Nice – a view she'd been waiting to experience for years.

The sea – in the late morning sunshine – a shining band of silver as far as the eye could see. Four stories below, the Promenade des Anglais – white pavements, palm trees, strolling tourists, open carriages and expensive cars – stretched for a mile in either direction.

On both sides, the white stucco facades of other terribly expensive hotels – each seemed to outdo the next in luxury and ostentation.

"What do you think? Quite something, isn't it?" said Harry, joining her.

"Everything you said it would be," said Kat, turning and kissing him. "And then some."

They stepped inside, into the cool shade of the room.

"And now you're deserting me to go and meet your spy," she said, smiling.

"Sorry. Wish I wasn't. In fact, I'd like nothing better than to spend the day snoozing on that rather glorious triple-sized bed with you in my arms. Maybe with a swim or two thrown into the mix."

"I know the feeling. Fascinating though young Roscoe was – boy – could he put the booze away. I'm exhausted."

She and Harry had stayed up shooting the breeze with the young American until the barman had finally asked if they could *please* let him close. Kat was still feeling a little worse for wear.

"I *should* be back around four," said Harry, slipping on his linen jacket and taking his valise from the desk. "Oh, do enjoy the shops."

"Dangerous words," said Kat. "I'll do my best to surprise you."

He walked over to her, gave her another kiss.

"Ah – even more encouragement to hurry back. By the way – I have dinner booked. See, I can do surprises too," he said.

Then, with a tip of his panama, he was gone, and Kat turned to her cases to unpack properly.

HARRY SAT IN the little backstreet café and ordered a *café au lait*, looking to anybody just like the typical tourist.

Which – right now – he was anything but.

Wyndham Groves arrived bang on time, and Harry recognised the tall, willowy Englishman the second he turned the far corner into the street.

The two of them drank coffee together for ten minutes, chatting innocently about cricket and rose cultivation (while making a mental note of every passer-by who might act too curious.)

Then they strolled to Wyndham's apartment.

But, instead of going in, Wyndham gestured to a little open-topped Peugeot parked outside – the car, the prettiest shade of sky blue.

"Thought we'd have lunch up in the hills, old boy?" said Wyndham, climbing into the driver's seat. "Hope that's okay with you?"

"Splendid," said Harry, joining him in the car.

An hour later, and they were sitting in a quiet garden corner of a tiny restaurant in Eze, with, Harry noted, a breathtaking view over the coast, marred only by the pile of work folders on the table between them.

Just two businessmen going through sales figures, Harry imagined they would seem to a casual observer. But Groves had been living in Tangiers for a year, and these "sales figures" were the details of contacts that might prove useful to His Majesty's Government, *with Africa – experts predicted – set to be an area of global interest and inner turmoil.*

Harry had barely met Wyndham before, but he warmed to him enormously as the meal progressed. The man was old-school and close to retirement, but he had surprisingly modern views and was all for Harry's – to some of his colleagues – unorthodox marriage.

"An American wife, working for the State Department?" Wyndham had said. "Well done, I say…"

"You'll have to meet her. I mean, socially and all that."

"Terrific."

Then, work done and bill paid, Wyndham drove back down into Nice – a little fast, Harry thought, on the winding road. Cicadas chirruped in the afternoon heat. Back outside Wyndham's apartment, Groves handed Harry the keys to the two-seater.

"Say – I've no need for the car this week, old chap," he said. "But I'm sure you and your wife could use it? Go ahead. All yours! I doubt you'll need to go above thirty, but, I'll tell you, she can fair fly round those hills if you've got someone on your tail!"

"I think," Harry said, with a smile, and nodding to the hills above Nice, "you displayed some of that speed up there."

"Ah yes. I do like pushing things a bit."

"But thanks for the loan. I will take very good care of her."

Harry took the keys as Wyndham extended them.

"Enjoy it. She can handle both the speed *and* the corners!"

With a nod, Harry got into the car, started it, the throaty engine under his control as he pulled away, and drove back to the Negresco.

What fun, he thought. *Shame I won't get the chance to see if she lives up to that billing.*

WITH THE CAR safely parked by the concierge team, he crossed the domed marble-floored reception area on his way to the elevator, looking forward to a quiet evening with Kat.

But it soon appeared that wasn't to be.

When he entered their suite, he could hear Kat in the shower. And, laid out on the bed, were her evening gown and his own tuxedo.

The quiet evening seemed to be vanishing before his eyes.

He went into the bathroom and popped his head around the misted shower glass.

"Guessing there's been a change of plan tonight?" he said.

"Yes. Your darling aunt called," said Kat, turning. "She's

22

invited us to a cocktail party in Antibes."

"Ah. Such a shame," he said, sitting on the edge of the bath and taking off his shoes and socks. "Was rather looking forward to a romantic evening, just the two of us."

"She said, laughing of course, that there was absolutely no refusal."

"That's my aunt."

He stood, and started to undo his shirt buttons. "Room for one more in there? I mean, I really should shower."

"I'm sure," said Kat.

"'No refusal', eh? Interesting turn of phrase. She tell you *why*?"

"She *did*, actually. There's a friend of hers in trouble."

"And she wants us to help out?"

"Mind reader," said Kat, handing him the soap.

"Amongst other talents," said Harry, stepping into the shower.

SEEING THE CAR, Kat grabbed the keys from Harry, and though it took her a few minutes to figure the Peugeot's controls, she soon had them flying down the coast road towards Antibes.

Wind in hair – the blue-green Mediterranean to their left in the late afternoon light, woods and mountains to their right, and the scents of pine and flowers heavy in the air – she felt like she was in a movie.

An hour later, and they drove past the ochre-coloured buildings of Antibes Old Town, and on towards a less densely populated area with grand villas and rolling gardens that led down to the sea.

The house was easy to find, and Kat turned into a sandy lane, joining a long line of cars filled with elegantly dressed partygoers.

"If we were to pluck the diamonds from around some of these graceful necks," said Harry, "I imagine you and I would be set up for life."

"You know, I'm glad we were dragooned into coming. This looks *amazing*."

They followed the other cars into a sweeping drive, past great fountains and perfectly cut lawns, to a long, low but expansive villa, lit by lines of flickering flares. Again, more movie-set than home.

From inside the house – or perhaps the gardens at the rear – Kat could hear the sounds of a jazz band and the buzzy chatter of guests.

"Your Aunt Lavinia certainly does mix in the right circles," said Kat as she parked, and they climbed out of the little car.

"And talking of mixing," said Harry, taking her arm as they joined the crowd climbing steps into the house, "I'd bet that bottom dollar of yours that the cocktails here will be out of this world."

"OH, AND SEE the little chap over there by the fountain, surrounded by women?" said Lavinia, as she led Kat from the house out onto a terraced garden where a jazz band was playing. "Pablo Picasso. He keeps promising me a painting, but – to be honest – I wouldn't know where to hang it at Mydworth Manor."

Kat saw a waiter passing and she took another glass of pink champagne from his silver tray.

"All these famous people, Lavinia – isn't it rather tiring?"

"Not at *all*, darling. One just treats them like anybody else. That's what they like, I *promise* you. Honestly, you should see some of them close up at breakfast. Dreadful complexions. The previous evening's wit having fizzled away in the morning light."

Kat had spent an hour being introduced to all of Lavinia's "housemates" as she called them. When Harry had told her Lavinia was "lodging" for the season with some dear old friends, *this* wasn't quite what she'd expected.

The "old friends" turned out to be the famous American socialites Gerald and Sara Murphy, and the "lodging", their extraordinarily beautiful villa, dubbed "Villa America".

The invites for tonight's party had gone out to a select gathering of the great and the good staying on the Riviera – and apparently nobody had turned them down.

"Oh look, they've launched more canapés, I absolutely *must* have another of those little pastries, they're divine," said Lavinia. Kat smiled and watched Harry's aunt sail back into the house.

She moved through the crowd looking for Harry.

Just then, an English voice at her side.

"Do you *play*?"

She glanced over to see a small card table in the corner of the terrace, and what looked like a game just finishing – a couple leaving – and the man who'd spoken, standing, shuffling cards, smiling at her.

Tall, relaxed, dark hair, smart white tux and a teasing eye.

The kind of eye that Kat knew of old, seeking out single young women at a party.

"Oh, I'm here just to have fun, not to win money," said Kat, smiling but not stopping.

"Stick around, you could do *both*," said the man, but she had already moved on, leaving him to his card game.

At the improvised garden stage, she stopped as the jazz band struck up another number, this time with a young woman singer joining them. The moment she began to sing, Kat was captivated.

Not only beautiful, with cropped black hair and dark eyes, but with a voice like velvet. Sensitive, purring, sensual.

"Simone Sorel," said Lavinia, arriving beside her with a plate of delicate pastries and Harry in tow.

"I say. She's amazing," said Harry, taking Kat's arm.

"*Isn't she?*" said Lavinia. "So sweet, too. And—" Lavinia's voice lowered some more "—she's *also* the reason I invited you tonight."

"Well," said Harry, "I wouldn't have missed her singing for the world, but, you know, it *was* quite a drive out here, Lavinia." Harry tipped his glass back and forth. "Not that I'm complaining."

"No, I meant you can hear her sing any time, Harry," said Lavinia. "In fact, she has a nightly spot at the casino in Nice." Then she turned to both of them. "But the *real* reason you simply must meet her, is for something entirely different."

Kat saw that Lavinia was now deadly serious.

"And that reason?" said Harry.

"Blackmail," said Lavinia. "Blackmail of the most sordid kind."

Kat saw her scan the partygoers, then turn back to them.

"Come with me," she said. "The Murphys have set aside a private room for us to meet. Simone will join us later. You see, there is somebody *else* you must meet first."

Kat looked at Harry – who shrugged, then plucked two glasses of champagne from another tray – and together they followed Lavinia into the teeming house.

Kat felt an unexpected chill as that word hung in the air. *Blackmail.*

4.

TRUE LOVE

HARRY WALKED WITH Kat and Lavinia through a pair of doors that clearly separated the public areas from the private.

They passed through a comfortable sitting room, along a quiet hallway into a small, dark study – drapes on the windows pulled shut – to where a group of armchairs had been arranged around a low coffee table.

In one of the chairs, Harry saw a stout-looking man, in his fifties perhaps, dressed in a crisp white linen suit with a bright kerchief in the top pocket, matching his red bow tie.

"Percy," said Lavinia, as the man stood to shake hands, one hand on a cane. "My nephew Harry, and his wife, Lady Mortimer."

"Percy Porter," said the man, and Harry felt the warmth of his smile – though he could see also a terrible strain clouding his face. "And do call me Percy."

"I shall leave you three alone, for now," said Lavinia, and she gently shut the door behind her.

"So, Percy," said Kat, the moment awkward.

Can't just jump in and say 'can you tell us about the blackmail'? Harry thought.

"Are you here for the season?" he said instead.

"I am. First time, you know. Extraordinary place!

Wonderful! Not at all what I expected."

"And are you here… alone?" said Harry, wondering if there was a Mrs Porter.

"Alone? Oh, right, I see. Yes. I mean no. Or rather, I *was* on my own. Came down from Manchester a couple of months ago. My wife – Lady Nantwich – was going to join me, but she has been, er, delayed. Although I am expecting her, I believe, in a couple of weeks. Yes – two weeks."

Harry could see that Percy Porter was deeply distracted. *So now to find out why.*

"My aunt tells me you have something of a problem, Percy?"

"A problem. Yes, oh yes… do I have a problem."

Harry waited for Percy to elaborate, but the man just stared into space. He carried on, slowly.

"She thought perhaps it was something my wife, Kat, and I might be able to help you with. Perhaps I should explain. We both have a… background, working with our separate governments abroad, in what one might call sensitive situations."

"Sensitive? Oh, I *see*… yes."

"Anyway," continued Harry as patiently as he could, "since we moved to England, we've helped out more than a few friends who have found themselves in, um, difficult circumstances."

"*Difficult circumstances.* Oh, that's me, all right. *Very* difficult circumstances."

Kat leaned forward, her voice steady, reassuring, Harry noted.

"Percy, can you explain what these 'circumstances' are?" said Kat. "We promise you that nothing will go beyond this room."

"And though we can't promise we can solve your *problem,*" added Harry, "we will do our damnedest to help – if we can."

"So, to start, why don't you tell us what has happened?" said Kat.

"What has happened?" said Percy. "I've got myself in a bit of a pickle, that's what's happened. A real pickle! Which is very ironic, really because well, that's my line – *pickles!*"

Harry peered at him, for a second confused.

"Percy's Pickles and Sauces!" said Percy. "Surely you've heard of us? 'Every mum's favourite', so the adverts go!"

"Of course! Harry enjoys your brown sauce with his breakfast, Percy," said Kat, "but I guess he never looks at the label."

"Oh yes. One of our top lines, that brown sauce," said Percy. "It's the molasses, you see. Secret ingredient. Takes the edge off the vinegar."

Then he seemed to remember the situation.

"Um, right, yes," he said, his face clouding over. "The business in hand."

Harry watched as Percy reached into a valise that sat at his feet, and pulled out two brown envelopes. Slowly, he opened the first, removed a sheet of paper and handed it to Harry.

"This came two weeks ago, left for me at my hotel in Cannes."

Harry needed only one glance at the stuck-on, cut-out letters to recognise instantly the classic blackmail style.

"And the photographs? Which I assume came with the letter?" said Harry, handing the paper to Kat.

"I destroyed them," said Percy. "I just couldn't bear to have them around!"

"Twenty thousand francs," said Kat. "A lot of money. What

did you do?"

"I paid it. As instructed."

"And then?" said Harry, already knowing the answer that was about to come.

"I got this just today," said Percy, removing a second letter and handing it to Kat.

"Fifty thousand?" she said. "And more photos too?"

Harry saw Percy nod.

"And have you paid?" said Harry.

"Not yet."

"Good," said Kat, and Harry caught her eye.

Well this is going to be interesting, he thought.

"LET'S GO RIGHT back to the beginning," said Kat. "And how about you tell us where the whole thing started."

She reached into her handbag and took out a small, leather-backed notebook and a silver pen.

Cocktail party or not, she thought, *this is an interview, and notes are very much in order.*

"Funny thing," said Percy. "It began right here in this house, on Valentine's Day, no less. Can't fault my timing, eh?"

And for the first time, Kat heard Percy Porter laugh. The sound more of a chuckle. Endearing. Warm. Engaging.

"Right out there, on that lawn," he said, nodding to the window where Kat could see fountains and flower beds falling gracefully down a perfect lawn to the distant sea.

"On that very spot I fell in love, with the most wonderful woman in the world."

And, as if on cue, the door opened wide, and Kat looked up to see Simone Sorel, the exquisite singer from the band – her pose dramatic, as if she were about to step on stage, the audience primed for her opening line.

"Percy, *mon cheri*," she cried, shutting the door and rushing over to him. Percy stood immediately to embrace her, hugging tight, eyes closed.

Kat looked at Harry, who shrugged and smiled at this unembarrassed display of affection. She waited as the embrace lingered, then finally the two separated. Simone turned her gaze towards Kat and Harry, then quickly back at Percy.

"Do they know? About us?" Simone said to Percy.

"I reckon they do now," said Percy, laughing.

"And are they going to help?" she said, as if Kat and Harry were not in the room. "They *must*!"

Kat wasn't sure about the singer who had just entered the conversation.

"Must" – *never a word she liked very much.*

"Help? If we can," said Kat. "Let's start again at the beginning, shall we?"

HARRY LISTENED AS Percy talked, the man's face growing florid as he remembered every – to him – precious detail of how he met Simone.

"Of course, I didn't think, I mean, an older gentleman like me, asking such a talented young woman to share his table or a drink? Foolish, I know."

Simone was quick to challenge that.

"But you had been coming to the casino for so many evenings! *Just* to hear me sing. It was *trés charmant*!"

Harry could see that Kat had her eyes trained on Simone as she spoke. Was she thinking what *he* was thinking?

Older man, younger woman.

Wealthy older man. *Struggling* young woman.

Not exactly a new tale.

But, he had to admit, Simone sounded genuine enough when she responded with warmth to Percy's story.

"Well, it was all a bit of a dream, least for me," said Percy.

"*Moi aussi!*"

"We started to spend time together, walking, talking, shopping – all on this wonderful Riviera!"

At this, Percy paused, his eyes bright. "Quite simply, my life had changed."

Simone still beamed at Percy. Then she saw him studying her face. Her smile faded a bit.

"You see, I have had a difficult life. Even to become a singer, here *sur la Côte*. So challenging. So much of a struggle. And this sweet, kind man—" she reached out and put Percy's left hand between her two hands, pressing it "—he understands me, *non*? For the first time of my life I feel – what is your word? – *appreciated*. Cared for in a way that I have never been."

Percy put a cap on the moment.

"I love her. Plain and simple."

And while Harry wasn't sure, he thought, *Who knows? Could be. Love comes in many forms.*

Unfortunately, the path chosen by Percy had brought him to this perilous, and potentially expensive, point.

He looked at Kat, knowing she must have a fusillade of questions ready.

And that she did.

"PERCY, SIMONE… thank you for sharing all this. Helps us

understand." Kat smiled and looked at Harry.

"You know, Sir Harry and I have found our own path to true love has been considered, well, a little shocking to some people."

"Really?" Harry said, grinning. "Now why didn't someone ever tell *me* that?"

Kat kept her smile in place, though this moment was not light.

Harry knew from seeing her in action that when she shared things – just like that – it was her way of disarming people, before diving into anything dark and disturbing.

In this case, *blackmail*.

"Why don't you tell us about that first message. The delivery of the cash? And maybe, if either of you," a look to Simone, "have any suspicions as to who would do this?"

Percy shook his head quickly. Simone did not follow suit.

If her life had been such a hard struggle, thought Harry, *the school of hard knocks, the young girl's guard would be up.*

"No," Percy said simply.

Kat responded by casually opening her notebook – pen at the ready. "You didn't hesitate to pay?"

"Oh, no. I was *horrified*." Percy lowered his voice. "I mean, the idea of someone taking pictures of us? At such intimate moments? Horrifying!"

Simone gave the man's hand a squeeze.

"And the arrangements?"

"Well. They followed in another message. I withdrew the Francs first thing in the morning, and then walked to the place indicated. It was an out-of-the-way bistro in Cannes. Sat at a table, ordered a café, placed my valise on the ground, also as instructed. Then, after just a very few minutes, I left."

Harry turned to Simone. "And Simone, you didn't go with Percy?"

"*Non*," she said, a hint of disappointment in her voice. "I had asked him, 'Please, let me come with you. You *must* be safe.' And who knows what such people might do."

Percy sniffed. "I couldn't permit that. Not at all."

Harry nodded as Kat continued.

"And then?"

"I thought that would be *that*. We'd be free. Of course, I knew I would have to sort out my personal life… all that. A quiet divorce. But *no* scandal. No terrible summons to appear before the board of *Percy's Pickles* to explain," his face reddened a shade, "my behaviour."

KAT NODDED AND let the embarrassing moment pass.

"I have a question," Harry said, standing up.

The move, perhaps designed to signal either the interview was at an end, or – Kat thought – *one last turn into unknown waters*.

Perhaps both.

"So neither of you have any idea at all who might have taken those photos? Why they decided to blackmail you?"

Percy looked away. But Simone… *Was she too quick, again, in the shaking of her head?*

Then the gentleman, looking dapper in his crisp summer suit, bow tie perfectly placed, cleared his throat. "That's just it. As I said, I do not. I've not been one for making enemies, even when growing the company. As to who discovered our wonderful *liaison* and decided to use it against me. Against *us*…" He shook his head. "I'm afraid, I have absolutely no clue at all."

Simone nodded at this. Then she, too, stood up.

SECRETS ON THE COTE D'AZUR

"I will be on stage again soon. I must prepare for my next numbers and get ready."

Kat stood up quickly. "Of course. Adore your singing."

"*Merci*," Simone said with a small smile. She squeezed Percy's hand and left the room.

Percy, though, seemed fastened to the luxurious chair, with its thick brocade and polished wood.

Harry walked to him, and put a hand on his shoulder.

"Percy. Perhaps – for now – we're done?"

The man looked up, with gentle but pleading eyes.

"And you think you'll be able to help me? Somehow?"

Kat walked over. "We will do our best. But blackmail? Well – we're not experts. You could involve the police?"

Percy was already shaking his head.

"No, no. Then, it all goes *public*. You can be... discreet?"

Harry smiled at that. "We will be. But I'm afraid whoever is doing this will keep it quiet only for as long as they think—"

"That I'm 'on the hook'?"

Harry nodded.

Percy turned from them, looking at the room's windows, framed with thick curtains.

"And, as to the next delivery? They want the money tomorrow!"

"For now, Percy," Kat said, "do nothing. Best to leave the waters undisturbed – the blackmailer thinking all will go according to plan."

"Yes, and we will be in touch," said Harry. "First thing in the morning. Once Lady Mortimer and I get a chance to plan."

Percy nodded, and Kat wondered if the man felt relieved. Or did this confirm his worst fears: that his goose was, indeed, cooked?

At which point, the door to the room opened and Lavinia slipped in. The jazz band could be heard – then Simone singing.

The song – appropriately enough – *"Am I Blue?"*

"Harry, Kat… the Murphys were asking after you. This *is* a party after all."

Percy stood up, hand clenched on the silver grip of his cane.

The shame of all this… weighing on him, Kat imagined.

"We're done here, for now, Aunt Lavinia," said Harry, clapping another hand on Percy's back.

"Go. Try to enjoy the evening. We'll do what we can."

Percy said a barely audible "Thank you", then shuffled out of the room.

When he was gone, Lavinia had a question.

"*Can* you do anything? I've grown rather fond of him over these last few weeks. He is such a *dear*."

"We'll see what we can do," said Harry. He nodded in his wife's direction. "Kat and I will need to have a little chat. Think she has a smidge more experience in such matters than me."

"Blackmail," Lavinia said. "Horrible."

Then Harry's aunt turned and started out of the room – out to bright lights, candles, music.

"But," she said over her shoulder, "do put all thoughts of that away for now? This is one amazing 'do'! The Murphys know how to throw a party. Oh, and there are even other Americans here."

Kat smiled at that, the word 'American' used as if it referred to a form of tropical bird.

"Anyone we'd know?" Kat asked in all innocence.

"Oh, I should think so. Both in their cups, I must warn. As usual. Scott and Zelda."

Kat stopped for a moment and looked at Harry.

The equally famous and infamous Fitzgeralds?

But all he said was, "Well then – welcome to the Côte d'Azur!"

5.

DEUX BOULEVARDIERS

KAT DROVE BACK, having had a glass or two less than her husband. The night had turned the slightest bit crisp, and she could look out to the Med, still and flat, glass-like, reflecting a new arrival suspended in the sky. A half-moon, cutting a bright, white roadway that led from the stony beaches straight onto what seemed the endless distance of the great sea.

A magical view, dreamlike, like none she had seen anywhere else in the world.

The road ahead – empty. Some way far behind them – the lights of another car.

Other guests from the party, she imagined, *heading back along the coast.*

And they talked – not only about what they had learned from Percy – but about the rather amazing party.

"You realise," Kat said, glancing at Harry, "that the gorgeous young man we spoke to at the end was the *danseur étoile* of the Paris ballet?"

"That fellow? He *did* look rather agile. I do have a question though."

"Yes?"

"That artist chappie, Picasso? What do you think women find so damned attractive about him?"

"Attractive?"

"I mean, are *you*, say, *hypothetically* attracted to him?"

"Piercing eyes. That's for sure. And he is one of those people that, when you talk with him, you feel all else has disappeared for him in the moment – save *you*."

"Ah. I really must get that skill under my belt."

Kat laughed. "Think you do just fine. Saw you talking to your share of the ladies."

"Well, of course. It was a party, after all."

"And your thoughts about the Murphys?"

"Interesting. Wealthy expats, lounging in their villa in Antibes. I didn't expect much, really. But the man, very bright. Paints too, you know. Has a show in Paris this autumn."

"And Mrs Murphy?"

Kat knew Sara Murphy's reputation as a beauty.

"Ah, well, speaking objectively and all—"

"Careful there, Sir Harry."

"She is indeed quite beautiful, and oh – I must add – smart as a whip as well. I like them both. Hope we see them again."

Kat took the great curve of the Moyen Corniche, the car handling the twisty road wonderfully. Nice, the old and new city, came into view. The promenade lit as if another party was going on right down there, along the sea.

The dome of the great Hotel Negresco lording it over the scene.

As they dropped down from the coast road into the edges of the town, she glanced in her mirror but the other car had gone.

Just before she got to the hotel where an attendant would somehow find a safe place to park the Peugeot, Harry turned to her.

"Tired?"

40

"God, yes. You?"

"Oh, that I am. But I think, with Percy's situation, maybe a chat and a nightcap? Outside, at the hotel's brasserie?"

Kat turned and looked out at the dark sea, with the shimmering white of the brilliant half-moon cutting through it.

"Yes. Bed can wait."

"That it *can*." Then adding. "Though one hopes… not too long."

And, slowing the blue Peugeot, Kat had to smile at that.

KAT WATCHED THE young waiter. He looked crisp in his white jacket, black pants and matching tie – as if this wasn't so very late at night.

He put down two round coasters, each emblazoned with an ornate "N", then placed the two drinks dead centre on each as if this operation was some test of cocktail marksmanship.

After an "Anything, else *monsieur, madame*?" and Harry's smiling "*Non, merci*", he left them to their small table, in a corner of the terrace of the Hotel Negresco.

They sat together with their backs to the hotel, the tall windows behind them open into the nearly empty hotel brasserie, the cool sea breeze making the curtains billow and sway.

Kat took in the view. There were still a few late-night revellers at the tables both inside and out here on the edge of the Promenade des Anglais, but she felt that they would not be overheard.

She examined the cocktail, a healthy orange peel clinging to the side of the delicate glass – a 'surprise' Harry had said.

"Okay – don't think I can guess what this is."

SECRETS ON THE COTE D'AZUR

"Thought I'd stump you, even with your years of experience."

Kat laughed. "Experience pulling 'pints' and pouring shots of Canadian Club."

"Ah, good old Canadian Club."

"Did the trick for most of my dad's patrons." She took a small sip. "Okay, I'm tasting whisky. No, *bourbon*. And sweet vermouth? Then... something else?"

"*Not too bad*. Bourbon and vermouth right, and amaretto is the hidden ingredient."

Another sip. "Delicious. What's it called?"

"*Un Boulevardier*. I even know the chap who invented it. Lives in Paris but he's one of your countrymen."

"Well done, I say."

"He named it after a little Parisian magazine he publishes."

Kat said the word again. "Boulevardier... perfect."

"Isn't it though?"

Only then did Kat turn away and look out at the Mediterranean. The moon, higher in the sky now, made the ripples on the surface shimmer and sparkle like a sea of jewels.

"Harry. So glad we're here."

She noted that Harry, while looking out at the dark sea, had turned quiet.

"You said you've been to the Negresco before?" she said.

He turned to her, taking his own glass in hand. Kat waited. Memories and talking about the past were not usually something Harry did.

"My parents brought me here, the first time. I was nine. A boy. Right to this great hotel. With the beach – the *plage* – and that pale blue water you could actually swim in."

"And were you a well-behaved boy staying in this grand

hotel on the Côte?"

"I do remember… I had a slight altercation with one of the bellhops. Something about running down corridors, bumping into people – unintentionally, of course." He took a breath. "I loved it."

And then she saw his eyes go back to that sea.

Of course, Harry had seen another dark sea, one like no other, many years ago. But that night, the water grey, cold, freezing – not at all like this.

The last night he saw his parents.

It was a memory that Harry had only mentioned a handful of times, and Kat, respecting that, never pushed. But she knew, despite her husband's humour and adventurous spirit, that, like the sea out there, there were much darker "waters" for him as well.

"Been thinking," he said. "Poor old Percy?"

"Yes?"

"Well, quite frankly, I'm not at all sure how we can help the fellow."

Kat took another sip of her Boulevardier, not wanting the delicious cocktail to vanish too quickly. *This might just be my new favourite drink,* she thought.

"Been giving it some thought as well," she said. "We had a few cases at the law office. But while I personally wasn't involved, I knew some of the Pinkerton people who laid a trap once."

"Pinkerton? The detective agency? I have heard they don't fool around."

"*That* they don't. So, yes, I do have an idea of how to maybe help Percy. Not without some risk. And even danger."

"There you go, *that* word again. Does seem to be part of our life together."

She smiled at him, his face now catching some of that milky moonlight as well. Then, checking nobody at the other tables might be listening, she leant in close.

"Okay. Here's the idea. It's simple, really."

6.

TO CATCH A CROOK

HARRY LISTENED ATTENTIVELY as Kat rolled out her plan.

"Tomorrow, first thing, we call Percy. Tell him that just as soon as he gets instructions for the 'drop' – where, when – he gets things in order to make the delivery."

"But he doesn't put real francs in the valise, surely?"

"*Au contraire*. Fact, he needs to make sure that he calls plenty of attention to himself at the Banque Populaire. And then, back at the hotel, if Simone joins him, she too sees all that cash."

"Ah, I see where you're going with this. The money has to be real... for a lot of reasons."

She laughed. "You *do* catch on. So, then, he lets us know where the location for the drop is, we get there ahead of time, park, wait, watch."

Harry nodded at that. "I do believe we're getting to the 'danger' part."

"Maybe. Percy leaves the cash. And when whoever comes and gets it, we follow them. If they know Percy, I doubt they'll suspect any funny business."

"'Funny business' as in him confiding in people like us?"

"*Exactly*. So, we follow. Maybe confront the person, or at least see where they go."

Harry nodded, but something about this didn't fit.

"Hang on. If we confront the blackmailer, he will still have the photos. Could still expose Percy – bring him down?"

"Always that risk. But in the cases I was privy to, when caught and confronted, the blackmailer – rather than face jail – turned over everything and disappeared."

"And no retribution?"

"Exactly. The blackmailed parties simply wanted it all to go away."

Harry took a last sip of his cocktail. "So, you imagine… maybe the same here? It is a gamble, though."

Kat turned back to the sea. She saw a lone fishing boat out there, bobbing as its mast and hull caught some of the moonlight. Perhaps pulling up nets with the evening's catch.

"A gamble, yes. But one I think we have to take."

She looked at Harry, his drink gone, hers with a bare drop left.

"Well then, seems we may have a busy day tomorrow," Harry said. He nodded to the nearby hotel doors with the gleaming brass handles, and extended his hand to her. "Shall we turn in, my brilliant partner?"

And Kat got up.

The evening, not quite over.

MORNING: A BRILLIANT sun overhead in a cloudless sky. And, just off Rue de Verdun, Harry watched the mid-morning crowds glide in both directions around the parked Peugeot – Cannes bustling.

He thought he had picked a discreet spot, away from the "drop" location. But now their car was engulfed by the tide of morning strollers – people shopping for dinner at the market, workmen hurrying to a favourite café for *un express*, children, led in a line as if they popped out of a storybook.

When they'd spoken to Percy in Cannes – first thing – he had already received the drop-off instructions: a typed sheet of paper slipped under his hotel door in the middle of the night.

The message abrupt: the name of a café – *Le Cochon Qui Fume*. The table number outside – four. The time – 11am. The instructions – *leave the money in a valise, take a coffee, go.*

Percy had initially protested at Kat's plan to use real money.

All that cash, the trip to the bank – *and just leaving it there, at the café?* He, too, raised the point – *couldn't some wads of paper do the trick?*

It was left to Harry to explain to him *exactly* why it should not be that way. He could hear Simone in the background.

Only then had Percy finally agreed to follow the instructions precisely, as if this wasn't a trap.

Off to the Banque Populaire, then back to the hotel, packing another valise with bank notes. And then – this probably terrible for the fellow – sitting in his hotel room, waiting for the appointed hour.

Harry looked at his watch.

"Nearly eleven," he said to Kat. "In your experience, are blackmailers punctual?"

She laughed. "I did warn you. My experience... limited. Percy knows the deal. Just gotta hope *he* keeps to the schedule."

Harry looked away, wondering if perhaps he should move the blue car, now looking out of place in the morning's throng.

His gaze, like Kat's, was fixed on the outside tables of the small bistro. One table at the far end of the bistro's outdoor space had a piece of shiny metal on it.

Probably, Harry thought, *signalling that it's "reservé".*

SECRETS ON THE COTE D'AZUR

The bistro owner: in on this deal in some fashion, likely given a few francs to keep table four clear.

"Come on, Percy," Kat said.

Harry guessed, this being Kat's plan, she felt responsible for seeing that it actually worked.

Then, down the road, he saw Percy heading for the café, walking more slowly than the hurrying crowd, cane in one hand.

"There we go," Harry said.

Percy wore a suit, of course: a white seersucker, with blue stripes, a bright white shirt with blue bow tie, his panama hat making it hard to make out whether his eyes showed fear. He looked out of place in these winding backstreets.

If it was my fifty thousand francs in the valise, I'd be damn worried, Harry thought.

"Okay," Kat said. "He sees the table. Sitting down."

Harry kept his eyes glued on Percy. He didn't so much sit on the red metal chair as perch there, as if ready to fly away at the first sign of something wrong.

A waiter, with a classic apron and equally appropriate mustachio, appeared. Percy said something; the waiter vanished.

"So far, so good," Harry said.

In a moment, the waiter appeared with *un express* on his tray, along with a small ceramic bowl with sugar cubes piled like blocks of snow.

Percy didn't touch the coffee. But he did reach into his pocket, Harry saw, and put down some coins.

Harry could guess, with all this, he was well out of his depth.

Then the moment…

The cup untouched, as well as the cubes of sugar, Percy

stood up. It was hard to see, but it looked like the valise had been pushed flush against the side wall of the café.

Percy adjusted his hat low, as if to shade his face – as though he was the culprit here. He stepped out onto the pavement and walked away down the curved street, heading back to the grand avenues and the promenade.

The instructions Percy had quoted were very clear on this point: *Do not look back, no matter what.*

And so, he didn't.

For several terrible moments the table was empty, the valise obscured, while Harry and Kat simply waited.

"Hang on," said Kat, leaning forward. "See that guy, near the tabac?"

Harry turned, looked up the street, to the nearby tobacco and newspaper store. A man stood there, waiting. Short and stocky, with tight-fitting pants, a jacket, and, on his head, a skull cap with goggles. If the fellow was trying to blend in, he was doing a very bad job.

"Looks like he's dressed for—"

But before Kat could finish that sentence, the man – as if some inner alarm had gone off – started quickly across the street, cutting through the throng of people, and it was all too obvious his target.

The bistro. The table.

"I do believe," Harry said, "we're about to get our 'pickup'."

He started the car, the next few minutes crucial to their plan.

He watched as the man walked through the sea of people, sun hitting his leather skullcap. After every few steps, he looked around. When he reached the pavement by the café, he stepped up close to the table.

And Harry saw him – in a flash – lean down, grab the valise, turn and head back.

"Things are about to get interesting," said Harry.

"As if they weren't before."

Harry let the car idle a bit as the man came back to the tabac, and then turned a corner into a side street.

"Okay – time to move."

Harry edged the car out into the centre of the road, but with the large number of people, he had to drive so slowly.

"Come on, come *on*," he said, the crowds not parting. Every second, the man – out of sight – was putting distance between them.

Harry moved the car forward, the small road just ahead, with the tabac at the corner, until the people finally moved out of the way, and he could slip out of first gear.

At the corner – down the side street – they saw him.

Just as he hopped onto a motorcycle.

"Uh-oh," Harry said, recognising the make of motorbike. "A Gnome Rhône."

Harry quickly hit the throttle as the man, now astride the machine, spotted them and, almost too casually, gave the bike a kick, wheeled left, and then rocketed down the street.

Harry threw the engine into second, then third gear. This whole situation – racing down a tight street – about to get dangerous.

He didn't take his eyes off the rider.

"It appears we have a *chase*."

7.

THE ADVANTAGES OF A TOURING MOTORCYCLE

KAT WATCHED AS Harry, both hands locked on the steering wheel except to shift up and down, stuck hard on the man's tail through the maze-like back streets of Cannes.

"Gnome Rhône?" she said.

"Yes. French built. A touring motorcycle. *Speedy*. Well, you can see *that*. Handles beautifully. Rode one in Morocco."

He took a breath as the bike did a near 45-degree turn to the right taking a corner.

"It's going to be hard to keep up with him," he said.

"But when he hits the open road, this car must surely be a lot faster?"

She saw Harry smile at that.

"Indeed. But for now, he has us outmatched."

Then another corner, this time to the left, over cobblestones wet from a nearby street cleaner, a man with bristle-brush broom, sweeping soapy water off the pavement into the cracks and bubbles of the old stones.

For a moment, Kat thought the rider would slide on the wet, slippery stone. And yes, she saw a bit of a wobble on his next sharp turn, *but no*.

The car handled the turn fine, though Harry had to shift up and down to keep the speed up.

"I do hope he's going *somewhere*," Harry said. "Looking forward to a chat with the fellow."

Another turn, and this time, right in front of them, only yards away: an old woman slowly leading a donkey pulling the smallest of carts, loaded with fruit.

"Harry!" Kat said, instinctively, as Harry hit the brakes, and came to a dead stop, just a yard from the woman, whose scowl matched that of her sleepy-eyed donkey.

"Oh, *come on!*" Harry said.

Ahead, Kat could see the biker – having hit this straight stretch – putting more distance between them.

Getting away with a valise with fifty thousand francs in it.

That was going to present all sorts of problems.

Harry rolled down the window and – though frustrated – Kat saw him smile, and, in as pleasant a Harry-voice as she could remember said: "*Madame, s'il vous plaît? Moi, ma femme, nous—*"

The woman did a dismissive wave with her hand as if she had no need of any "story" tied to the entreaty, as she yanked the even more reluctant donkey to the side, making just enough room for the Peugeot to pass.

"Merci!" Harry said loudly, as he hit the throttle, the rider now a dot in the distance.

With the car now flying even faster, Kat could feel every bump in the ancient cobblestone road.

"Harry… bit fast?"

He nodded.

"Afraid we don't have much choice."

And, indeed, Kat saw that they were gaining on the motorbike, now on this straight section and Harry going full out.

Until…

The bike slowed, nearly stopped, and took another turn. This – no high-speed, death-defying angle…

But something slower, much more careful.

What is it? Kat thought.

In seconds, they reached the place where the bike had turned, to see an alleyway maybe three or four feet wide. Too narrow for the car, but wide enough for the Gnome Rhône – which had stopped no more than thirty feet away, the engine turning over, the rider, turning slowly to face them.

"Whatever is he up too?" said Kat.

And then she saw the rider reach into his jacket and slowly pull out…

… a handgun, and point it right at them.

Everything suddenly seemed to happen in a rush – Harry throwing the car into reverse as they both dropped down into the seats of the Peugeot – then the crash of the gun going off and the zip of a bullet over their heads.

For a second, there was just the sound of the Peugeot engine – then she heard the sharp growl of the bike and knew it was off and away, flying up the alley.

She looked at Harry. "You okay?"

"Never better," he said. "You?"

"*That* was no warning shot," she said. "Just a bad aim."

"Indeed."

She gestured at the alley, and together they climbed out of the car, walked to the alleyway.

In the distance, she could see the bike disappearing.

"Can we get to where this comes out?" she said, turning to Harry. "Catch up with him there?"

"Can try. Of course. But I think – until we have a little more firepower – perhaps discretion is the order of the day."

Kat looked back down the empty alley that had ended the chase.

"He got away."

"*Indeed.*"

"With all that money."

"Yes."

"How will we tell Percy?"

Her husband had no answer.

HARRY WAS WILLING to call Percy's hotel, but Kat thought, *My plan, and my job to deliver the bad news.*

They had driven straight back to the Negresco, and now sat together at the desk in their room, Harry leaning in close to the earpiece.

Listening to the moans and wails of the sweet man who had found what he believed was the love of his life, Kat realised that there was absolutely no way to soften this blow.

The money was gone. And the threat of a terrible scandal was still *very* much there.

"Um, Percy, can you handle today like any other day? Take your walks? Have your usual lunch?"

She paused, shooting a "this isn't going so well" look at her husband.

"Sir Harry and I will put our heads together. Least we know how the pickup is done, the getaway vehicle, and… What? No. There was no licence. The man must have masked it."

Another look to Harry.

Then she thought of something to be discussed with him as soon as the call was over.

But for now…

"Is Simone there with you? Oh good. Um, what will she be doing?"

Kat heard Percy explain that Simone would go back to her hotel to rehearse for her show that night.

"Very well. We will not abandon you, Percy." Then, because she felt she had to, Kat said. "We're *so* sorry."

To which, before hanging up, Percy simply said a very dull and hopeless "Yes".

OUT UNDER THE canopy of the Negresco's cheery bistro on the beach, an hour later, Kat had ordered a citron pressé and a croque-monsieur, not that she felt hungry at all. For Harry, *une bière*, and an oeuf mayonnaise.

After all, it was now lunch time in Nice.

"You're quiet," she said to him.

"I can't stop blaming myself for losing the damn bike."

"Well, no way we could know that he'd hit one of those alleys."

"That donkey cart lady wasn't too much help either."

She grinned at that, even though − considering the circumstances − this was not a time for any levity.

"And, as you told Percy, without a licence number there's no way to trace the motorcycle."

"So, we will need do something else. Any ideas?"

"Not immediately," Harry said

The waiter hurried over, silver tray with their drinks and food, put down quickly before flying back into the bistro.

Kat looked down at her croque, perfectly browned, the melted cheese bubbling on top of the toasted ham sandwich.

SECRETS ON THE COTE D'AZUR

Wonder why they don't make these back in the States? she thought.

"You know, Harry, that motorcycle man *knew* he was going to be watched."

Harry speared a chunk of egg, with a dollop of mayonnaise on it.

"I agree. Not only all set for a getaway – but I think that alleyway was planned all along too."

"Gun ready, if needed. You think he thought we were police?"

"Don't know. Don't *think* so. Though he probably was on watch for that too. But, yes, I believe you're right, Kat. He knew someone would be there, waiting, watching."

She cut a small corner of her croque. The gruyère nicely strong, the ham salty. *Perfect.*

"We both know there was only one person – beside Percy – who knew what was going to happen."

Harry took a sip of his beer.

"Simone," he said.

"Right. All kind of classic, right? Older gentleman. Showgirl. Money and blackmail."

"Does seem to fit. So now…?"

"Think it's time we learned a bit more about our cabaret singer," Kat said.

"Shouldn't be difficult to find out where she's staying. Could drop by her hotel, have a little chat?"

"True," said Kat. "But maybe better – we go see her show tonight. Find out who she mixes with, ask some questions, put out some feelers."

"We know where that is?"

"Didn't your aunt say she has a regular spot at the casino?"

"You're right. Okay, let's make a night of it. Good excuse to pop the old tux on."

"Business and pleasure – my perfect date," said Kat.

"*Exactly.*"

"Afterwards, how about we follow Simone, see where she goes?"

"*Cherchez la femme*, eh?" said Harry, laughing.

"True," said Kat. "If she's involved, sooner or later, she'll lead us to the man on the Gnome…"

Harry laughed again. "*Gnome Rhône.* And don't ask me why they call it that!"

Kat cut another piece of her sandwich and popped it into her mouth. Dabbed her lips with the napkin.

"And this afternoon?" she said.

"Why don't we tootle down to Cannes, talk to Percy properly? On his own this time."

"Good idea. Maybe learn more about how he and Simone hooked up together. Particularly, who found *who*?"

"Mustn't forget we've got one other lead."

"The café?" said Kat, remembering the blackmail instructions.

"Exactly. That waiter must have been slipped a few francs to hold the table free for Percy – and the money drop."

"Okay – so why don't we split up? You take the waiter, I take Percy to tea?"

"That's a deal. I think I might drop in on Wyndham first, see if he'll tag along with me – supplement my schoolboy French."

"Good idea," said Kat. "Was also thinking – what you said earlier about firepower… You think Wyndham can help in that area?"

"Ha! Oh, I'm totally sure of it. Usual preference?"

SECRETS ON THE COTE D'AZUR

"Yes, Colt automatic – if he can lay his hands on one."

"On this coast? A doddle, I would have thought."

"Let me guess. That word means 'no problem'? And you?"

"Oh, a good old service revolver will suit me just fine, and I imagine he already has one *in stock*, as it were, that he can lend me."

Kat laughed, thinking, *Can't be many couples know their partner's taste in handguns.*

"Well then, I think we're done here," she said, finishing her citron pressé and putting her napkin on the table. "Ready?"

"Ready," said Harry, draining his beer and standing.

Kat waited for a second as he slipped a couple of notes under the plate, then she took his arm, and together, in the sunshine, they walked back up the boardwalk to the promenade.

They looked, to any passers-by, just like an ordinary couple with a leisurely afternoon to spend, mooching around the stores.

Little do they know, thought Kat, smiling to herself.

8.

A SURPRISE VISITOR

HARRY PUSHED OPEN the double doors of the little café, *Le Cochon qui Fume*, and let Wyndham go ahead of him.

Inside, the place was dark and smelled of wine, coffee and stale cigarette smoke. In the corner, Harry could see a couple of what must be regulars, playing cards, a bottle of Ricard and a jug of water on the table between them.

A scratchy ballad played on a small radio behind the bar, the sound tinny but fitting the dreary setting, Harry thought.

Otherwise, apart from the elderly barman slowly wiping glasses without enthusiasm, a cigarette drooping from the corner of his mouth, ash about to collapse, the café was empty. *No sign of the moustachioed waiter.*

Harry pointed to some stools at the bar. Wyndham nodded, and – sitting beside Harry – ordered two cafés, his French abrupt and fluent.

Harry didn't say anything. This place – and their mission – much more in Wyndham's wheelhouse. *Good to have him here.*

A few minutes later, the barman slid the cups of coffee across the bar. Harry listened as Wyndham struck up a conversation with him – Harry's own French rusty, but good enough to get the gist.

Turned out the barman was in fact the owner. And the

waiter with the moustache? His name: Jean-Marc. He was in the storeroom sorting crates.

So, non, sorry messieurs, but you cannot talk with him today: he is far too busy to disturb.

Harry saw the bar owner smile and shrug, and knew the real meaning of that shrug from far too many negotiations in bars and alleyways around the world. He looked at Wyndham, then reached into his wallet and took out a crisp fifty franc note. Slid it across the bar.

"*Bien sûr. Peut-être*, this might help?" said Harry.

The man rubbed his chin. Harry produced another note.

"Aha, I do believe I hear Jean-Marc now," said the owner suddenly in perfect English, picking up the notes from the bar, then folding them and slipping them into the top pocket of his waistcoat. "He must have finished. I shall tell him he has *visitors*."

As the man disappeared to the back of the bar, Harry looked at Wyndham and smiled.

"Based on that exchange… kind of an expensive town," Harry said, as they slid off the stools to follow the owner to the storeroom.

KAT SAT ON an antique chaise longue in the salon of the Carlton Hotel, Cannes, sipping the most perfect mint tea and taking in the extravagant surroundings.

She glanced across at the reception desk. She'd sent a message to Percy's room that they needed to meet, and now she had been waiting for nearly half an hour.

The hotel was clearly busy – *perhaps that explained the delay?* She was about to call a bellhop to investigate, when a female voice came from behind her.

"Lady Mortimer?"

Kat turned to see an elegantly dressed woman, standing peering at her, a handbag on one arm, a folded silk parasol in one hand.

Kat stood.

"Yes," she said, surprised.

The woman smiled and held out her hand to shake.

"Lady Alice Nantwich. You know my husband, Percy."

For a second Kat was confused – then she remembered.

This was Percy's wife! Not expected for another two weeks!

"Er, yes, indeed," she said. "I do believe I've had the pleasure of meeting Mr Porter—"

"*Please*," said the woman, taking the seat next to Kat's. "There's no need for any pretence." She gave a weary shrug and smiled. "I know *everything*. Or, at least, as much as I need – or want – to know!"

"I'm not sure I understand," said Kat, careful not to give anything away in what might be a *delicate* situation.

Kat saw Lady Nantwich laugh.

"Don't worry, my dear, I'm not going to bite," said the woman, looking around the salon. "Now, where's that waiter? Before we get down to business, I absolutely *must* have a cup of tea. And then we shall have *such* a nice chat, I'm sure."

Kat watched Lady Nantwich signal to a passing waiter, place her order, then sit back in her brocaded armchair, hands neatly entwined, a patient smile upon her face.

This, thought Kat, *is turning into one interesting afternoon.*

HARRY SAT WITH Wyndham on beer crates in the cramped

storeroom of the café – a cracked and musty window above the shelves, open to a dim back alley, offering the only illumination.

Leaning against the wall, facing them both, was the moustachioed waiter Jean-Marc. Harry could see the man was nervous: a sheen of sweat on his upper brow; tell-tale wiping of his hands on his drink-smattered apron; and frequent glances at the half-closed door into the café.

Le garçon knows something is "up", thought Harry.

At first, the waiter – claiming to speak only French – had denied even being at work the previous day. Then he switched his story – said, oh yes, sure, he had been at the café, but couldn't remember the well-dressed Englishman at table four.

Then he flipped again, agreed he'd served him, but knew nothing at all about the reserved table.

The sweat on his brow kept pace with the changes to his story.

And now he was refusing to answer any more questions.

Harry looked at Wyndham.

Time to change tack, he thought. *In fact, time to play an old game that rarely fails.*

"This is going nowhere," Harry said, as if Jean-Marc were not even in the room.

"Agree," said Wyndham.

"You think a couple of hundred francs will loosen his tongue?"

"Possible. If not, a night in the cells should work. We've got enough on him to turn him over to the gendarmes."

"True. But once he's in the system, he could be there for months. Not even his family will have access, so unlikely we will."

"Ah, yes. The sluggish wheels of justice. But we don't have

a choice, Harry," said Wyndham, playing along nicely to Harry's game. "Come on. Let's call the police from the bar telephone. Soon as they pick up our friend here, we can catch the next train back to Nice."

Harry nodded, then shoved his crate to one side and stood up as if to go, Wyndham rising too.

They got as far as the door, when Harry heard the word he'd hoped for.

"Wait!"

And in English, too. No surprise there.

He turned, to see Jean-Marc step past them and shut the door urgently.

"You do not need to call the police. *Non!* I'll tell you what I know."

"A name?"

"Yes, a name. Everything. Just keep me out of it. These guys – they're bad news – if they hear about this, I'm dead."

Harry looked at Wyndham, then back at the waiter.

"Okay, *mon ami*," he said. "Start talking."

KAT WATCHED LADY Nantwich as she poured tea into the delicate china cup, added just a touch of milk from a silver jug, and took a sip.

"So refreshing," said the woman. "Though the French never do get the milk *quite* right, don't you find? Always warm. Don't understand *that* at all!"

"I'm more of a black coffee person," said Kat.

"Ah yes, of course," said Lady Nantwich, nodding as if in forgiveness. "You would be. An American thing, yes?"

Kat didn't agree or disagree with that view.

Percy's wife leaned forward. Almost as if they were old friends, catching up.

"I know we have *matters to discuss*, but isn't this the most *splendid* morning? I arrived so late last night, in the dark – such a tiring journey, those trains! But the weather right now in England – heavens! It's so unutterably awful I simply couldn't take another day of it! Rain, rain, and more rain! But here – the climate – so delicious, *n'est-ce pas?*"

Kat nodded, a small smile. Blackmail and her marriage at stake, and here they were discussing the weather.

That must be an English thing, she thought to herself.

"I must say though, Percy *was* surprised to see me. As ever." She laughed. "He attempted – in truth, rather pathetically – to pretend he hadn't been up to his old tricks again. But, as I'm sure you appreciate, a wife always *knows* these things. Knows them instinctively, don't you find?"

"Old tricks?" said Kat. "I'm afraid I don't—"

"This girl, Simone? A cheap showgirl *again*. How dreadfully predictable and tawdry. You'd think after all these years he'd tire of empty-headed entertainers. A librarian would make a pleasant change! Or perhaps a timid little bank clerk? Ah well. I suppose at least with a singer or a dancer one knows precisely what one is dealing with… and paying for."

Kat stayed silent, trying to come to terms with Lady Nantwich's version of Percy Porter and his great romance – so different from the story he had presented to her and Harry.

The wife could be completely right, she thought.

"Of course, what makes this particular little episode so *unfortunate* is the rather nasty additional ingredient of blackmail. Horrible word. And handfuls of money – *pffffft* – out of the window."

Lady Nantwich took another sip of her tea.

"You see, until now, dear Percy's peccadillos have remained completely private. We've managed to keep them *in the family*, as it were. Society and – more importantly – the company board of directors, remain unaware of his *proclivities*. And it must remain that way or the consequences for our future? Well – all too dire to imagine. And to that end—" she reached across and placed her hand briefly on Kat's knee "—I must say, I am absolutely *overjoyed* to hear that you and Sir Harry have become involved. But now, we have but a few minutes before Percy joins us, so you really must tell me *exactly* what you have discovered so far. And perhaps, between us all, we can sort out this *odious* little mess."

Kat thought quickly. Apart from the issue of confidence, until she knew more, she certainly wasn't going to reveal any suspicions or plans.

Not that she and Harry had much of either.

"Lady Nantwich, I must say, you clearly have a very forgiving nature. Not many spouses would be so, er, understanding?"

"Please, call me Alice," said the woman.

Kat smiled, nodded.

"And I'm Kat," she said. Then she sat back on the chaise longue. "As I was saying – to be honest – I'm surprised you take Mr Porter's affairs so lightly."

"Oh, I'm far too long in the tooth to waste time fretting about what my husband gets up to. As long as it is contained. However, in this case... *blackmail*... it appears I have no choice but to get involved."

"Does Percy know that we are having this conversation?" she said.

"That he does."

"And he's told you what our involvement is? My husband and I—"

"Indeed. I know you and Sir Harry have a little *experience* in this line of work. And that you tried to follow the suspects – but failed."

Kat nodded. *This was not the time for excuses.*

"To that end, I'm sure you're wondering how we proceed? I mean, with me now on the scene, as it were," said Lady Nantwich. "So, let me say now, I am completely happy with Percy's decision to *enlist you* to the cause."

"I see."

"You have my full support. And I assume you are expecting another – even higher – demand from the blackmailers?"

"We are."

"One question though. Do you think this *Simone* woman is involved?"

"We're keeping an open mind to all possibilities."

"Yes. Well, I wouldn't keep it 'open' for too long. A floozy like that? She's probably in it up to her camisole! What next then?"

Kat decided to ignore the slur on the young singer.

"Well, that's why I came here this morning: to discuss our strategy with your husband."

"Not expecting the wife. Well, good," said Lady Nantwich. Then she looked across the salon to the doors. "I see no reason for that to change at all. As long as you're happy talking to both of us?"

Before Kat could answer, she saw Lady Nantwich turn. "Ah, look – here's our easily duped *Lothario* now."

Glancing across the bustling room, Kat saw Percy sheepishly

edge into view at the double doors and peer around looking for them.

"Just one more thing I should add," said Lady Nantwich quietly. "Percy asked me not to discuss his previous dalliances with you, and I agreed. The man clearly still has at least a modicum of dignity, so I feel we should respect that."

Kat didn't reply. This whole situation was plain *curious*.

She watched as the portly Percy threaded his way through the other tables and finally reached them. He stood rather meekly, shuffling from foot to foot.

"Ah, um, Lady Mortimer," he said, smiling weakly, "I see you have met my wife."

"We've been having a lovely chat, haven't we, *Kat*?" said Lady Nantwich, smiling at Kat. Then she turned to her husband.

"Do join us, darling. I've ordered you a tea, just as you like it: stewed."

Kat watched as Percy Porter sat on a red velvet armchair next to his wife, and perched on the edge, his knees together.

Despite the saccharine words, he looked to Kat like a man who had just received a life sentence.

9.

A TRIP TO THE OLD TOWN

HARRY STEPPED ONTO the pavement outside Wyndham Groves's apartment building, tipped his panama hat low against the late afternoon sun, and checked his jacket was buttoned.

Not due to any chill though.

He smoothed the material. He was reassured to have the borrowed Webley revolver, concealed and snug in its holster. But he was well aware he was taking risks, carrying the weapon on the streets of a French city.

Though, with what he and Wyndham had learned from the waiter in Cannes, he knew there was simply no choice.

What was the famous line? *Don't bring a knife to a gun fight.*

After waffling, Jean-Marc had named the biker: a thug from Marseilles with the nickname "Capo" and, according to Wyndham, a police record as long as his arm.

One very nasty – even *deadly* – mobster.

Capo had appeared one morning a few days earlier, given his instructions to Jean-Marc, and warned him to look the other way when the pickup was made. There'd been no payment up front, but the waiter had known well enough not to argue.

Harry had slipped the waiter some francs and told him to phone the Negresco if Capo turned up again.

Not that he expected it. *If there was a third pickup, it would surely happen at a new venue.*

Most likely with the same MO.

On the quick train journey back to Nice, Wyndham had filled Harry in on what he knew about Capo – and the fact that he had moved up the coast to the Riviera from Marseilles in the last year or two.

The English spy had been surprised at Capo's involvement in a blackmail attempt.

"According to my contacts in the police, Capo specialises in burglary, extortion, a little armed robbery, breaking and entering when the mood takes him," he'd said, "but I've never heard him linked to blackmail."

Harry guessed they must be looking at the "muscle", not the "brains", of the operation. He also knew that if they were to find the blackmailer, Capo was the only lead they had.

So, now he was heading for the Old Town to check out the notorious drinking den that Wyndham had heard Capo frequented.

The Liberty Bar.

Late afternoon, mid week, Harry knew he'd be lucky to even glimpse the man, but at least he could "case the joint" as Kat would say.

Ready to drop in later, maybe with Kat at his side.

After all, by then the Colt that Wyndham had "ordered" from his friends in the local underworld, should have arrived at the Negresco, with a handy box of ammunition.

How surprised the receptionists would be if only they knew what was in the pretty package behind the desk addressed to Lady Mortimer.

THE WALK FROM Nice station heading towards the sea was such a pleasant stroll, past stores and apartments, restaurants and *salles de thé*.

But as soon as Harry entered the Old Town, the mood changed.

Here, the streets were clustered tight together, tiny bars and cafés jostling for customers, shoeless children playing down dark cobbled alleyways, streams of people crammed tight, faces grim. Life on the Med not a romp, but a struggle.

He could see, straight away, the bitter poverty that existed just yards from the glamorous hotels of the Promenade des Anglais.

Remembering Wyndham's directions, he threaded his way deeper, easing through jostling crowds, aware that his linen suit easily made him stand out from the locals.

But, at the same time, he guessed that even the city's most respectable inhabitants often frequented some of these streets in search of forbidden fruits.

At the cathedral, with its shining new memorial to the Great War, he crossed the little square, took Rue Rossetti, then a sharp left into Rue Droit, the smell of cooking from all the cafés mixing with swirls of cigarette smoke and the dank aroma of open drains.

And, there ahead, he saw the Liberty Bar – an ancient sign hanging crooked above a faded red door, and only a small window in a wall.

He walked past, quickly glancing at the window but seeing nothing – the interior obscured by a tattered curtain.

Must be one hell of a dreary boite!

He knew that simply going inside would never work. *How am I going to play this?* he thought.

And then – amazingly – he heard a familiar rumbling sound in the distance.

A Gnome Rhône.

Getting closer.

It had to be Capo!

Quickly Harry stepped into the doorway of the nearest shop and pretended to be interested in the tiny window display of grim-looking medical supplies.

He heard the bike closer now, approaching down the Rue Droit, the engine snarling as it sped down the narrow street.

Just as it passed him, he pulled his hat low.

Out of the corner of his eye he could see the rider as he flew by.

There was no doubt. It was the same man from the day before. Leather cap pulled tight… goggles.

Capo.

And in the angled shop window, he had a good view of the bike's reflection as it stopped sharp in front of the Liberty Bar, just twenty yards back down the street.

Harry expected the engine to be turned off, but, instead, Capo stayed astride the machine, and gunned the motor once, twice.

A signal?

Then Harry saw, in the reflection, the door to the bar open and a figure appear. He took the risk and turned to see better, still pressed tight into the shop doorway.

The man who had emerged from the bar: tall, in a faded suit, a battered Homberg covering his head.

Too far away to get a good view of his face.

But certainly looking as if he – like Harry – didn't belong here.

SECRETS ON THE COTE D'AZUR

Harry watched as Capo reached into his leather jacket, removed a bulky package, handed it to the man, waited.

The man looked nervously up and down the Rue Droit.

Harry pulled back, then – waiting a moment – again peered round the doorway.

To see the man, assured no one was studying him, rip the top of the package, check the contents, then nod.

Capo nodded too, head bobbing as if he was muttering something. Then he flicked the bike into gear. And, with a guttural roar from the engine, the gangster spun the machine around and came back up the street.

Harry spun round again, pressing tight against the window as the bike sped past. Inside the shop, Harry noticed a short man, with an elaborate moustache, a smile on his face as if close to luring in such a well-dressed customer.

Harry smiled back, hopefully signalling: *Sorry, only window shopping.*

Then he turned, just in time to see the man with the package walking away – so fast – and then disappearing round the far corner.

Damn!

Harry raced down the street, and stopped dead at the Rue Rossetti, looking carefully left around the corner.

And there he was – the tall man.

Maybe a hundred yards away, walking as fast as he could up the steep hill.

Harry followed, keeping a distance, dodging in and out of doorways if the man paused or looked around.

Harry knew this ancient street. He remembered from a trip years ago as an innocent tourist, walking the whole of the *Vielle Ville*, heading up this steep hill to the old castle and gardens.

Ahead now, he could see the man passing through the garden gates and then taking the stone steps fast.

Harry kept having to pull back, being more exposed here as they left the crowded streets below, quickly crossing the cobblestone road to be in shadow. If he went too fast, the man could double back and he'd be seen.

Careful, careful, Harry told himself.

But he knew he couldn't wait too long or he risked losing him completely.

He went through the gates, climbing the zig-zag steps that girdled the hillside, almost expecting at each blind turn to come face to face with what he now assumed must be the blackmailer.

Harry was glad he had his gun. Though he hoped he wouldn't have to use it. Helping his aunt's friend, that was one thing, but gunplay on the castle grounds? *That was something else entirely.*

Now the steps became a rough, rocky pathway, the turns further apart, but still climbing steeply; Harry, breathing heavily, beginning to sweat in the early evening heat.

Until, at last, he reached the hilltop, and stepped out onto a narrow, tree-lined lane. Behind him, he knew, would be the most amazing view back across the Baie des Anges.

Certainly no Bay of Angels today, he thought.

To his left, he saw the entrance to the ancient cemetery – to his right, the path to the castle gardens.

But no sign of the man, and a decision to be made: which way to go?

Why had the blackmailer come up here? Did he know Harry was on his trail? Or was this just experienced trade craft – the work of a professional criminal, always careful to cover his tracks?

Harry knew the cemetery to the left was a maze. If the man

had gone in there, it would be impossible to track him without being spotted. He had no choice.

He took the right turn, through the gardens, slowly walking past families, tourists, locals, lovers.

Trying to look as if he might be a casual tourist and not someone chasing a blackmailer!

All the time looking, looking for the man with the package.

But when he reached the viewpoint, a little knot of tourists taking photos, waiting for the sunset, he realised that he had lost his quarry.

Or rather, his quarry had "lost" him.

He stopped, took out his silk handkerchief, mopped his brow, and took in the amazing scene; the red roofs, the blue-green dark sea, the red hills in the far distance and the lowering disc of the Mediterranean sun.

But even this fantastic view gave him no pleasure.

Only frustration.

He had lost the damn blackmailer.

10.

A NIGHT ON THE TOWN

"DIAMONDS OR PEARLS?" said Kat, stepping onto the balcony of their room, where Harry stood staring at the moonlit sea, a crystal glass of neat whisky in his hand.

The air outside felt soft and warm to Kat. She watched Harry turn and consider the difficult question for the required few seconds – then he nodded to the pearls she held in her right hand.

"Weighty question. I think, keep the diamonds for our last night, don't you?" he said.

"Aha, our last night? Sounds like you have a surprise for me?"

She stepped forward and gave him a kiss, then turned with the pearls round her neck so he could do up the clasp.

"Oh, do I ever," he said. "All I have to do is work out exactly what it's going to be."

She laughed and turned around.

"You still feeling angry with yourself?" she said.

"Oh, not now," he said, kissing her gently. "Seeing you looking like this always does the trick."

"The whisky helps, I bet," said Kat.

"That it *does*," he said, laughing.

They stepped back into the room, and Kat took one last look

in the mirror as Harry drained his glass, then put on his white dress jacket.

They had booked a table at the casino cabaret, definitely an excuse for dressing up to the nines: Kat in her favourite long, midnight-blue dress, Harry in whites.

"What I can't fathom," he said, "is how I lost the blighter. He simply vanished!"

"Maybe he spotted you? Had some place to hide?"

"It's possible. I think he slipped into the old cemetery – a complete maze, unless you know your way round it."

"Okay – sounds to me like it was plain old bad luck then," said Kat. "And anyway, you must admit – a stroke of *good* luck turning up at the café just as the handover was taking place."

"Yes. Maybe. If it *was* the handover. Might have been a recipe for his dear old mum."

Kat laughed. "From the guy that took a pot shot at us?"

"Ha. That nice gentleman, Capo."

"Well, you certainly had more success than me. All I got was two hours talking fashion and London society with Lady Nantwich. Oh, and English weather as well."

"Not a topic to take lightly *that*. But not a peep from Percy the whole time?"

"Oh, he joined in with a pithy comment every now and then, but, in the end, I didn't get a single minute alone with him to get to the bottom of the story of him and Simone. I mean, that *is* why I went to see him."

"Sounds to me like Lady Nantwich didn't want that to happen."

"Right. That's exactly how it felt," said Kat. "And, call it instinct, Harry... something's not quite right there. But I can't put my finger on it."

"Oh, if I know you, Lady Mortimer, sooner or later, you will," said Harry, picking up his hat and dusting it.

"Harry – we need to decide on our next steps," she said. "I mean, if we're going to help here at all."

"Indeed," said Harry, "Though, until the blackmailers make the next move, I think we're stymied."

"*If* they make another move. And what about Simone? Perhaps a background check is in order."

"'Floozy', you said Lady Nantwich called her? Well, she sings amazingly for a *floozy*. But, yes, no harm in that – as long as we're careful not to alert her."

"Let's put that on the list for tomorrow, then. And take the evening off. Deal?"

"Deal," he said, stepping forward and kissing her.

Kat picked up her velvet clutch bag, popped the catch and took out the pocket Colt.

"What do you think?" she said. "Small, but it is still a weight. And I doubt we'll find ourselves in a shoot-out at the casino."

She knew Harry wouldn't be bringing his revolver – hardly a good fit under a dress jacket.

"You're right," he said. "Let's have a proper night off. Cabaret. Champagne. No handguns."

She laughed. "Yes! And perhaps just a teeny-weeny play on the roulette table?" she said, putting the gun back in the desk drawer.

"Why not? When in Rome, or a casino *sur la Côte*," said Harry, opening the door for her and following her out. "After all, the only *extravagance* we've had so far has been those two croque-monsieurs. Time to push the boat out, I say!"

"Whatever that means, Sir Harry. Sounds wonderful to me."

And, taking his arm, they headed for the Art Deco elevator down the hallway, Kat feeling a thrill, an excited anticipation, at the upcoming night on the town.

HARRY HELPED KAT out of the cab, and turned to take in the casino at the end of a short pier that jutted out into the dark sea, lit brightly against the starry sky.

The great building was already buzzing with guests arriving and leaving: cars and stylish horse-drawn carriages lined up on the promenade. Harry could hear the sound of a jazz band coming through the tall open windows of one of the restaurants.

He took Kat's arm, and together they joined the crowds strolling down the pier, then climbed the broad steps of the glittering casino into a great glass-domed reception hall with shiny marble floors, sparkling chandeliers, the place lively with visitors from all over the world.

Hard *not* to feel excited at all this.

As they crossed the hall towards the cabaret room, he felt a tap on his sleeve, and, as he turned, a familiar voice too –

"Hey Harry! Kat! Well, how about that!"

There – in dress suit and black tie – stood Roscoe Burns.

Their charming grifter from le Train Bleu! Here!

"Roscoe!" said Kat, and Harry saw her plant a kiss on the young American's cheeks, French style.

He shook Roscoe's hand, then made a fuss out of checking his jacket pockets.

"Just making sure my wallet's still here," he said, smiling. A look to his wrist. "My watch too. Okay – all good!"

"Guess I deserve that," said Roscoe, grinning. "But, you

know, I've gone straight. Just like I said I would."

"Got a job, huh?" said Kat, not hiding – Harry thought – a hint of doubt in her voice. "Somewhere in town?"

"Well… no," said Roscoe. Then he pointed to the doors to the gaming rooms. "I'm working *here*. As a croupier. Good with cards, you see."

"You're kidding me," said Kat. "I mean – you ever done it before?"

"Hung around the tables often enough," said the young American. "For other purposes, to be sure. But, I thought, how hard can it be?"

"Let me guess," said Harry. "You wrote your own references."

"And excellent they were. Would have taken way too long to get them posted from New York. Hey it's just putting a little oil in the wheels, way I see it."

"Well, we must drop by your table after the show," said Harry. "Though I'll be keeping my eyes on you."

"Ha! Don't worry! And no special treatment – even for pals," said Roscoe.

Harry laughed. "Wouldn't dream of it!"

Then Roscoe nodded towards a big poster of Simone that hung on one wall.

"You gonna see Simone Sorel tonight? What a voice! A real star – she's gonna go far."

"Oh, we already saw her, briefly, the other evening," said Kat. "And – I agree – an amazing talent."

Harry heard the band start up in the cabaret, and took Roscoe's hand again.

"Well – we'd better grab our table. Good to see you again, young man."

SECRETS ON THE COTE D'AZUR

"You too, Harry, Kat," said Roscoe. And Harry watched him turn and head off towards the gaming tables.

"That boy is going to go far, too," he said. "I don't doubt it. Question is… where?"

"I know," said Kat. "Long as he sticks to the straight and narrow."

Harry took her arm again, and they made their way into the bustling cabaret rooms, where a full-on jazz band was getting right into its stride.

THE MAITRE D' led them to their table, perfectly positioned in a quiet corner away from the stage, and Harry ordered a bottle of Pommery – fast becoming their drink *du jour.*

"What time is Simone on?" said Kat, as they scanned the menus.

"Closing act of the show, I think," said Harry. And, when the champagne had been poured, he raised his glass to hers.

"To the Côte d'Azur!" he said.

"And all its secrets!" said Kat.

They sipped the champagne, then turned to watch as a line of barely clad dancers filled the space in front of the band as the show began.

"Well, that's something you don't see every day in Mydworth," said Harry.

"Or even the Bronx," said Kat, and Harry laughed.

DINNER LASTED TWO hours, and Simone was – as Kat had expected – incredible. Her set effortlessly slid from big band number to intimate ballad – her presence seducing the whole room.

Finally, after two encores, the singer headed backstage and Kat leaned close to Harry.

"We got time to check out the tables? Or shall we pick up a cab back to the hotel?"

"Ah, tempting. But the night is yet young, yes? Come on!"

Kat leaned across the table, gave him a kiss.

"I'm *so* glad I married you," she said, getting to her feet. "You always want to do what I want to do!"

"It's my greatest quality, you know," he said.

He joined her, and, arm in arm again, they walked through the restaurant and out into the great domed lobby. At the double doors into the casino, she paused.

Inside, the gaming room was packed: roulette tables, baccarat – the crowds around some of the big tables two or three deep. Croupiers calling out; people laughing, cheering; waiters bustling past with trays held high above the crowds; champagne flowing…

She turned to Harry.

"You know, it's way too busy in here. Let's not get any chips. Let's just observe."

She nodded to a gallery dotted with spectators that ran around the high-ceilinged room, and together they climbed the red-velvet-carpeted steps until they were above the throng, looking down on the dozen or so tables.

A waiter brought them champagne, and Kat leaned forward against the balustrade to watch.

"Look at the roulette table over there!" she said. "That chap with the girl on each arm? Looks like he just won a fortune!"

"I can't imagine why he's so popular. How about that white-haired fellow on the vingt-et-un?"

Kat looked to where Harry was pointing, and saw a frail old man dithering over his decision, the rest of the table smiling patiently as he squinted at the cards in his hand.

Kat laughed. "And look! There's Roscoe," she said, nodding to another table in the far corner.

"He looks just the part," said Harry. "Oh – I do believe that's Simone, isn't it?"

Kat followed his gaze, and picked out the beautiful singer, now changed into another evening gown, threading her way through the crowd below, taking kisses and compliments at every turn.

She watched as Simone ended up at Roscoe's table. The crowd parted to allow the young star through, and she came to a halt behind one of the players whose back was to Kat and Harry.

Kat saw Simone lean in to the man as he played, one hand on his shoulder, saying something into his ear. The man half turned to answer – and then *Kat recognised him.*

It was the tall card player who had spoken to her at the party in Antibes.

"Harry?" said Kat. "Sorry. Night off and all. But I *know* that guy – the one Simone's talking to. He was at the party the other night. Was rather forward, in fact."

"Oh really?" said Harry, and he looked more closely at the far table. "Made a pass at my dear wife, did he? Well now, I really should get his measure! Ah yes, now I see him – well, well. I do believe I've seen him before too."

"From the party?" she said.

"*No,*" said Harry. Kat heard a change in the tone of his voice – this was serious. "*Not* from the party."

Kat turned to him.

"What do you mean?" she said.

"The man down there, whispering with Simone? He's the same chap I chased through the Old Town this afternoon."

"What?" said Kat, trying to make sense of these new connections. She looked back down to the table. Simone had now slipped away.

"But if he knows Simone, that means—"

"Indeed. I do believe we're back on the clock, my dear Kat."

And Kat wondered if it might have been a mistake not *bringing the Colt tonight.*

11.

A LATE NIGHT VISIT

KAT THREADED HER way through the crowded tables, picking up a glass of champagne as a waiter passed by, glancing up to the balcony where she could just glimpse Harry in the shadows, looking down.

The plan had been hers: *get close to the man, find out what she could.*

Harry hadn't argued. He knew it had to be done – and there was always the risk that the man would recognise Harry from today.

Whereas – even if he remembered her from the briefest of meetings at the party – he shouldn't be wary of Kat. Quite the reverse, even.

As she neared Roscoe's table, she saw him momentarily look up and notice her. Quickly, she pressed her fingers to her lips as if to say *Shhh, you don't know me.*

Roscoe looked back to the cards – not even a nod, but she knew he'd got the message. Closer now, she slipped through the lookers-on until she stood right behind the man from the party.

She saw he was the focus of the crowd's attention. He seemed to be doing well – very well.

A massive pile of chips was stacked by his cards, and, as the game progressed, and the cards flew, she saw his movements were slick.

Almost… professional.

This was a guy who knew how to gamble – and clearly loved it.

She watched and waited. The whole table silent, engrossed – a big play now apparently under way.

Roscoe dealt a card from the stack.

All eyes on the mystery man. What was he going to do – hit or stand?

She saw him make his mind up, a nod to Roscoe who smoothly flipped the next card.

And then a cheer as mystery man won – a stack of chips pushed his way to join the mountain already there.

"Well played," said Kat, stepping closer to him.

"Merci, madame," said the man, scooping up his winnings. Then he looked up at her, his eyes sparkling.

"Aha. If it isn't the lady who likes to have fun."

"Absolutely. No law against it."

"If there were," he said, holding her gaze, "I'd help you break it."

Kat smiled at the man's flirtatious tone. Then he turned and nodded at the cards, as the dealer went to work.

"You always take big risks like that?"

"All the time," he said. "You play?"

"Not tonight."

"And what do you do… Miss… Mrs…?"

"Kat Reilly," she said, *so strange to use her maiden name again.*

"Cedric Latimer," said the man, smiling and playing a card.

"Pleasure to meet you, Cedric."

"Pleasure's all mine, of course," said Latimer. "Are you down for the rest of the season?"

Kat played along. "Maybe. Maybe not. I get bored so

easily."

"Well, I'm sure we can do something about that. A little nightcap later perhaps?"

"I do like nightcaps. Where are you staying?"

"The Winchester. They have an awfully civilised piano bar. Lots of quiet corners."

"Sounds… romantic."

"What? Don't you *like* romantic?" he said.

"Oh, I don't know. I do have a party to go to."

"Perhaps later? Post party, as they say?"

"Maybe," said Kat. "When will you finish here?"

"Two? Three? I have a launch, moored on the end of the pier. We could go for a spin round the bay."

Kat shrugged. Time to look like she was playing hard to get. *And, after all, she now had what she needed.*

She looked around at the other tables, as if deciding where there was more reliable fun to be had.

"Oh – I see some friends," she said. "I think the party beckons."

"See you later, Kat Reilly."

"I did say 'maybe'."

"Quite the free spirit, aren't you?" said Latimer, looking up from his game again and smiling.

"You'd better believe it," said Kat.

And with a swirl of her dress, she turned and headed through the crowd and out.

Thinking, *Not a bad performance there.*

HARRY PAID OFF the cab outside the Winchester Hotel and stepped onto the pavement where Kat waited for him, in the shadows under a palm tree.

As soon as Kat had left the gaming rooms, they'd rushed to the taxi rank, headed down the promenade, straight to Latimer's hotel.

The plan was simple: with Latimer away from some hours, break into his room somehow, search it, find either the money or evidence.

Harry looked at the Winchester. Still lit up and busy, though the crowds were certainly thinning. He checked his watch.

"One o'clock," he said. "Let's assume the worst: our new friend has a couple of bad hands and packs it in, comes back to his hotel early."

"Hoping for a rendezvous with a certain femme fatale," said Kat, swishing her long dress.

"And not knowing that *that* is completely my prerogative," said Harry, taking her hand and kissing it.

"So, what do you think?" said Kat. "In and out of the place in half an hour?"

"At most."

"Two of us searching, shouldn't take too long."

"How shall we play it, Kat Reilly?" he said.

"You like surprises too, yes?" said Kat, laughing.

"Well, that I do."

Together they left the shadows and walked up to the grand entrance of the Winchester Hotel.

"PLACE DOESN'T LOOK *too* shabby," Harry said as they paused at the foot of the polished marble steps up to the hotel doors. "It would seem our Mr Latimer does relatively well at the tables – and whatever else it is that he does."

SECRETS ON THE COTE D'AZUR

"Like blackmail?"

"I imagine, with the right associates, a fast motorcycle and a gun, one can generate a tidy income."

"Have to remember – we don't have any solid proof of that."

"*Yet*. Now, you said you had a 'surprise'."

He stepped aside as a well-dressed couple walked by them and through the hotel's polished wood and glass doors, gleaming with the reflected glow of the nearby streetlamps.

Then he turned back to Kat and saw her smile. If there was one thing his wife wasn't short of, it was confidence.

"Okay, nothing ventured, right?" she said. "So, here's what *you* are to do…"

And she leaned close as if whispering details of further adventures on a romantic evening, but, in fact, laying out her plan.

HARRY HAD STROLLED to the edge of the pavement as if looking for a taxi, leaving Kat alone.

She waited a moment, then walked up the marble steps, taking care with her high heels.

A doorman, dressed as if for the chorus of an operetta – all gold braids, red velvet jacket, and ruffled shirt – pulled the main door open with a warm smile and a cheery "*Bonsoir madame*."

Yes, thought Kat. *Madame.* The French, always checking for the tell-tale sign of a ring, and the correct appellation: *madame or mademoiselle*.

She smiled back and entered the spacious lobby, the floor covered with a thick blue rug matching the sea outside, the edges trimmed in gold.

At the desk, just one person on duty. This suited her plan.

Add another employee, and that would double the chances for difficult questions. To make sure that she didn't get trapped in French, nuance flying out the window, she would begin with English.

Of a most American sort.

"Good evening," Kat said, smile in place. The desk clerk – with his carefully slicked down hair, perfectly round wire frames and a dark pencil-thin moustache – looked up.

Hotel like this, he has to speak English, she thought.

"Ah, yes, madame. A *very* good evening to you. How may I assist you?"

Clever. The man obviously knew she wasn't a guest.

"Yes, I think you can. You see, I'm an—" She paused, looked away, lowered her voice. "—*acquaintance* of Mr Cedric Latimer."

The desk clerk kept his smile in place, eyes fixed on Kat.

Her plan banked on the fact that Latimer's pastimes and pursuits – gambling and philandering – were well known.

"And, you see, he is still at the tables." Kat broadened her smile even further. "Having quite the night of it."

"Indeed, madame? That is excellent news."

"I *know*! Anyway, he asked me to meet him in your lounge. But with his streak of luck, I figured, that might be a while. So… I was wondering if I might freshen up, so to speak, in his room. Wait for him there?"

At that, Kat noted two things: the man's eyes narrowed, the request sending some small alarms through his mental roster of responsibilities.

But also – with a quick glance to one side – she spotted Harry enter the hotel, and stride determinedly to a corridor just off the lobby. Walking, she saw, with the speed and directness of someone perhaps heading to the elevator or in search of the lobby's phone.

Either way, he was in the hotel.

Kat continued: "I'm sure Mr Latimer would be so appreciative. This is shaping up to be quite a *special* night."

Kat tried to project – with her smile, her own eyes widening a bit – whatever meaning the desk clerk would apply to that last phrase.

But it still brought no nod from the man – this on-duty night *captain* of the hotel and its many floors of elegant rooms and suites.

And so, she played her last card.

"I could, of course, have you ring the casino, call Mr Latimer away from the tables. Though – not sure he'd like *that* much."

At that – facing a beautiful woman planning on an evening's engagement in a lucky man's room – the clerk nodded.

He kept his own voice low as if they were now in this together.

"Very well, madame." He raised an arm over his head and snapped his fingers with a crisp sound that brought a bellhop, all of five feet tall, hurrying over.

"Louis here will take you to the room."

"Thank you!" Kat said, genuinely appreciative.

After all, this little scheme could have gone either way.

"I will certainly let dear Cedric know later how you helped me, Monsieur—?"

"Thibaut, madame. I shall be here *all* evening should you, or Monsieur Latimer, require anything else at all."

Then, with an elegant turn to the wall of keys behind him,

Monsieur Thibaut grabbed what must be a master key and passed it to the bellhop.

"*Chambre huit-cent-trois,*" the desk clerk said. With a final smile to him, Kat turned and followed the small bellhop, towering over him as they made for the cage-like elevator.

Wonder how many times he's performed this particular little chore? she thought.

THE BELLHOP OPENED Latimer's door, and Kat pressed a few coins into his hand, then slipped inside – the room still dark – and shut the door behind her.

One part of the plan was still left. And it could all fail, if somehow Cedric did cash in, take his winnings, and sail back here early.

Which would make for an interesting encounter to wriggle out of.

She waited a few moments until she could be sure the bellhop had taken the elevator back down to the lobby.

Then she flicked on the main light and took in the room.

Large, with heavy Victorian furniture. An immense bed. Two floor-to-ceiling french windows, whose open curtains swayed from the sea breeze outside.

Quickly she walked over to the windows. They shared a narrow balcony with an iron rail. Eight floors below, she could see the sea and the promenade – street lamps still lit. She pulled the curtains tight, so no light might be visible from below.

Then she turned, and hurried over to an elegant mahogany desk in the corner of the room. Opened a drawer, and saw a small stack of hotel stationery. She took out an envelope, hurried to the door, and slid it under the door *halfway.*

This plan: not infallible, but it had worked for her before.

KAT STOOD IN front of the wide-open doors of the room's closet, which was filled with an assortment of day and evening wear, all neatly hung. Cedric was quite the dandy, it seemed.

Where to start? But then, a knock.

She went to the door, and opened it a fraction.

"Yes?" she said.

"Appears you dropped something," came a familiar voice.

She opened the door wider, and Harry slid in, envelope in hand.

"You know, what you did down there at reception?" He waved the envelope. "There is no way that would ever work for a man."

"Wasn't really sure it would work for me."

"Really? Swanky joint like this? Think they'd have Latimer's tastes down to a 't'. Beautiful woman on the romantic Riviera, and all that."

She watched Harry look around.

"Spot anything yet?" he said.

"No. Just started."

"Well then, to paraphrase the bard, *if it be done, best be done quickly.*"

Harry walked to the writing desk and started pulling out the drawers one by one, while Kat went into the bathroom. A marble sink with a gold-plated faucet, the towels hung neatly. Otherwise nothing.

Then: "Hey, Kat, look what I've found."

And she hurried back to the room. Harry held up the wastepaper basket from under the desk. She watched him pull out a small square of newspaper with odd chunks – here and there – cut out of it.

"Yesterday's *Le Figaro*," he said. "Full of holes."

"Used in the blackmail notes?" Kat said.

"So it would seem."

"Well – that seals it, doesn't it? Latimer's involved."

"Indeed. Though the photos and money are the real prize. You checked the wardrobe?"

"Was about to start when you knocked."

Harry nodded and walked over to it, carefully sliding the suits along the rails.

"Well. Looks like Cedric is planning for a long stay, with all the assorted outfits one might need. Shoes too. I say – see that hat?"

Kat came beside him and looked to the top shelf. A worn, rumpled hat with a bowl-like shape.

"That's what he wore today up in the Old Town," said Harry. "Trying to fit in with the locals, I imagine."

Kat went to the other end of the closet and pushed the clothes to one side, to reveal – set flush into the wall – a small, but very solid-looking safe.

"Aha," she said. "If this room has any secrets, this is where they'll be."

12.

SAFE SECRETS

HARRY BENT DOWN next to Kat to get a better look at the wall safe – its combination wheel and lever looking impregnable.

"Now, if I had collected a sack of cash today," said Kat, "I think this is *exactly* where I'd put it."

"Agree," said Harry, putting a hand on the metal safe. "I must say, though, damn thing looks rather secure."

He turned to look at Kat who, from her expression, appeared more confident than he did.

Not surprising: he knew that in her "diplomatic" work for the US State Department, she'd had training in safe-cracking. And, once or twice on cases, that training had come in handy.

"Right then," he said, "I think here's where I bow to your greater experience."

He saw Kat smile as she pushed close to him. "Need a bit of room to work. If you could…?"

Harry edged out, as Kat leaned close to the safe, putting her cheek next to it.

For a moment, the only sound was her fingers *slowly turning the combination lock.*

"GETTING ANYWHERE?"

Kat looked up at him. "Think I'm hearing the tumblers

click. A little quiet would help."

Harry nodded, and ran his finger across his lips as if zipping them.

She gently turned the wheel: forward... back... Then, at last, she heard a soft "click". She grabbed the metal handle of the safe and yanked it down – *and the wall safe opened.*

"Ta-da!" she said, and gave Harry a wink.

"I am *continually* impressed by you, Lady Mortimer. Yet another skill you must teach me. So, what's our prize?"

Kat peered into the safe, reached in and pulled out an envelope.

Her first thought: *Too small to hold the cash from today.*

"Nothing else?" asked Harry. Kat shrugged and shook her head.

Then she opened the envelope, to reveal...

Stacks of negatives. She took one out.

"Is it–?"

In answer, she held up the negative close to him, so that – facing the room light – they both could see the reverse image. A man. A woman.

Clearly clutching each other tight.

Difficult to see exactly their state of dress. But enough for her to imagine.

"The blackmail photos," he said. "But – damn it – not the money. I guess we keep searching?"

But, before Kat could answer, she heard a sound, a key, scrabbling in the door lock.

"Uh-oh," said Harry, his voice turned urgent, a whisper. "Quick – you hide in here."

The key rattled more, followed by a substantial click.

Kat mouthed the obvious question as she slipped into the

closet.

"*And you?*"

But Harry had shut the closet door and was gone.

INSIDE THE CLOSET, Kat heard noises. Cedric walking out of the room, into the bathroom, the sound of water running in the basin, followed by his footsteps returning. Then another sound: the phone's receiver being picked up.

Followed by a clackety noise: the rotary dial spinning, a call being made.

Now she leaned forward, an ear tight to the door to catch as much of the conversation as she could.

"*Hello. Yes. Tonight? Best not, I think, don't you? Discretion, right? What? Oh – yes. Everything is set for tomorrow. Doubt the old fool will play around at this point.*"

She wished she could see Cedric talking. All his smarmy charm and flirting from before, now replaced with a different tone. Edgy. Chilled. Determined.

And obviously planning yet one more blackmail note, one more pot of cash.

Tomorrow.

She noticed a small gap in the louvred closet doors and edged closer so she could just see a sliver of the room – but Cedric wasn't visible.

Clearly the person Cedric was talking to – whoever it was – must be in on it. Not only that, but that person *might* be key to where the money was.

The tens of thousands of francs that were nowhere in this hotel room.

"*Right, then. Best you get back to that. We're close now. Troubles almost over. Tomorrow. What? Yes, usual place after the pickup."*

The solid *clack* of the handset being put down. Through the gap in the door, she saw Cedric cross the room again.

For a moment, she thought he would come straight to the closet and begin undressing. And, despite a small forest of clothes on hangers in here, there was no question he'd spot Kat and her shimmering blue dress.

Not many good explanations for that!

And what about Harry? she thought. *What if he's under the bed?*

But then she heard steps. The room door opening again, then quickly shutting tight.

Cedric leaving.

Probably thinking he could go down to the hotel lounge and – if it was his lucky night – meet the woman in blue for a secret rendezvous.

Kat waited a few seconds, and then stepped out, still with the envelope of negatives in her hand, scanning the room for where her husband might be. She crouched down – peered under the bed.

Nothing.

She saw the curtains billowing with the steady breeze off the Med.

Hope he's not hiding behind there, she thought.

But the bottoms didn't quite reach the carpet and Harry's shiny dress shoes would have easily stuck out.

So where was he?

She went to the open french windows, and out onto the small balcony itself, but her husband wasn't there either!

She stepped forward to the iron rail, not daring to imagine what she might see, eight floors below.

But then – a familiar voice.

SECRETS ON THE COTE D'AZUR

"Er, is the coast, as they say, *clear*?"

She turned and saw Harry standing calmly on the next balcony a yard away.

"There you are," she said. "Thought maybe you'd decided to climb down."

Harry clambered up onto the rail and leapt across the dizzying gap. "Oh, I'm not *that* reckless. Climbing buildings is best left to the experts, in my opinion. So, has the blighter gone? Thought I heard him talking?"

"Yes. Phone call. And I'll tell you what I heard. But first – we'd better get out of here – in case, when he finds himself alone in the hotel lounge—"

"Ah yes, his assignation with that beautiful American... *up in smoke*."

Kat took Harry's hand and led him to the room door. "Must be a back stairway for staff."

"And ne'er-do-wells."

"Oh, that's *us* all right."

"Don't want to bump into Latimer on the way down."

And, once out in the hallway, they headed briskly down the plush carpet to the back stairs, designated "staff only".

13.

TO CATCH A BLACKMAILER

BACK AT THE Negresco, Harry pushed open the door to their suite and Kat went ahead, kicking off her shoes as she walked through to the bedroom.

"This footwear is killing me."

"Quite appealing as an accessory," he said, joining her in the bedroom. "But, I must admit, those heels *do* seem rather impractical."

"Big day tomorrow," she said, as he undid the zip of her dress.

"I'm starting to think every day on la Côte is a big day."

He tossed his suit onto a chair, and slipped into pyjamas and robe.

Then, while Kat changed, he headed back into the main room and rustled up two quite beautiful cut-crystal glasses, each with a few fingers of the whisky from the small rolling bar.

"*Tchin-tchin*," he said, tapping Kat's glass, as she joined him, now dressed in her own silk pyjamas, and – he knew – looking far more elegant than he did. Those pyjamas? Dressy enough to wear out, in his opinion.

He watched her take a sip, then they both settled into a pair of leather armchairs by the window, and Kat filled him in on what Cedric had said.

"Okay, so he definitely spoke to someone 'in' on the plan – and they agreed to meet up after the pickup 'as usual', he said."

"Hmm, *as usual*, eh? Male? Female?"

"Couldn't tell."

"And you're sure it wasn't Capo?"

"Definitely. Sounded like he was talking to an equal. Or maybe even the person pulling the strings."

"But no indication who?"

"No. Only that everything was being arranged for one more pot of cash – tomorrow."

Harry raised a hand. "'Course, *we* have the negatives. Could be the dreaded evidence against Percy is now safely in our possession."

"Well, yes. But Cedric doesn't know that. Unless he checks."

"True. But there is also another problem."

"Yes?"

"The money. All right, we may have the damning negatives. Might be others out there. Maybe not. But all that money… We really need to find out who has it."

"And how to get it back?"

"Precisely," said Harry. "Thoughts?"

"The person on the phone, could have been Simone, you know. Playing poor Percy while working with Cedric."

"To get the cash?"

"Right."

Harry checked his watch. "Getting a bit late for Percy to call. Feels like the next pickup is going to be tomorrow afternoon, earliest."

"So." Kat took a last sip from her glass. "To bed, I think. And in the morning, how about we call on Simone?"

"Great minds. Had that thought myself. If she has the

money, maybe force it out of her?"

"Easier said than done."

"True. *That* is the way with so many things, isn't it?" said Harry, finishing his drink too. "Now, I do believe you mentioned something about bed?"

AS HARRY GUESSED, early next morning they got a call from Percy. Another blackmail note had indeed arrived, promising, one last time, more threats and the largest demand so far: one hundred thousand francs.

Harry convinced him, yet again, to get the money and follow all the details. Percy reluctantly agreed. He was heading out soon, he said, and would do just that.

The rendezvous was apparently scheduled for later in the afternoon – somewhere in Nice.

Harry had decided that everything would be exactly the same as for the earlier pickup.

Except for one vital thing.

Instead of Harry and Kat staking out the drop location – yet another small café – this time they would get into position to trail Cedric.

With luck, he would pick up the cash from Capo same as last time – and if he was then handing the money to an accomplice, they might finally discover who that was.

"It's a plan," Harry said, as they grabbed a quick coffee in their room.

"That it is. And it's all we've got," said Kat. "*Unless* we get lucky with Simone."

THE TRIP TO Antibes in the little blue open-top took barely half an hour – Harry loving the run along the coast, the sea bright and sparkling under a perfect blue sky.

The morning streets of Antibes, jutting away from the amazing coast, so different from the bustle of Nice.

Narrow, with small shops and even smaller cafés.

People moving slowly, as if trying to get their day going.

Men with buckets of water and rough bristle brooms cleaning the sidewalks and streets, stirring up smells from the previous night's oysters and *filets*.

Other locals seated at the tables of small cafés – either a café au lait in front of them, or *un express*; probably depending on what hour of the morning it was for the patron.

"Could do with another coffee myself," Harry said. "All this exercise. Apart from the endless magnums of champagne and the late-night cocktails, I think doing this, er, investigating in the Riviera, is *much* healthier than in our little village."

"I'm just glad to be in some street clothes," Kat said. "Felt like a Christmas ornament last night."

Harry laughed at that. "Best ornament I ever saw."

She shot him a look, grinning.

Finally, they arrived at Simone's apartment building – the address supplied to them by Wyndham, from one of his "helpful local contacts". The building was nondescript, save for a leering gothic head marking each floor, and, at the top, some full-sized stone creatures standing guard with a nod to the great gargoyles of France's countless churches and cathedrals.

No doorman, Harry could see. That was good.

Inside the lobby – filled with the scent of a dozen different dinners from last night – a very helpful directory listed all the rooms and residents.

"There she is," Kat said. "S. Sorel. 237."

"Which is actually what you'd call the third floor."

She turned to him. "You do realise I have worked in a number of foreign capitals?"

"Right-o, mustn't forget that."

With no elevator, she led the way to the stairs.

WHEN THEY REACHED Simone's floor, Harry noticed someone midway down the long corridor. A young man, standing in a doorway, talking, nodding. Too far away for them to hear anything.

Could be nothing to do with Simone, he thought. Still, he edged back into the staircase, with Kat following.

Then the man turned and started heading in their direction, an envelope in hand.

"Okay," Harry whispered. "I recommend that we saunter down there as if we live here."

Kat took his arm and did exactly that as the man in the hallway approached.

Harry took a quick glance as he neared. He was young with long dark hair, wearing the clothes of a labourer – maybe someone who worked in a factory or a farm.

That envelope – a standard business one – held tight, as if important, valuable.

As the man passed – he bumped into Harry clumsily.

"Excusez-moi," said Harry, instinctively, and they kept moving – Harry checking the room numbers, soon realising that the young man had indeed been at Simone Sorel's door.

Harry reached out to knock on the door, and then heard

footsteps approaching fast from behind them.

He turned, to see the man just a couple of yards away, flying at them both, fists raised high, his face twisted as he shouted: "*Anglais! Je vous tuerai!*"

KAT TWISTED SIDEWAYS, instinctively throwing up her hand in protection as the stranger barged into both of them.

As she fell backwards, she saw Harry take the brunt of the blow on his chest, staggering backwards, the attacker bouncing against the side of the corridor, before lunging forwards again.

But, this time, she and Harry were ready.

As the man charged, Kat swung her foot out low, tripping him – and, as he lost his balance, Harry caught the spinning assailant and rammed him hard into the wall.

In a second, Harry had one arm against the back of the man's neck, his hand clenched around the man's other wrist, pulling his twisted arm upwards.

The man cried out in pain, just as the door to Simone's apartment flew open and Kat saw Simone appear, a look of horror on her face.

"Let him *go!*" cried the singer, and, she too, now launched herself upon Harry, beating her arms on his back.

Kat stepped forward quickly, and pulled the woman away, spun her round, pinning her arms to her side.

"Simone! Stop! It's us."

For a second, nobody moved or said anything. All four of them, just standing, panting, shocked at the sudden explosion of events in the narrow corridor.

But before Kat could say anything more, she heard a voice from the doorway behind her.

"Simone, *ma cherie*? What on earth is going on?"

She turned, to see a familiar face peering round the doorway of Simone's apartment: *Percy*.

"Well isn't this, er, a lovely surprise," said Percy, blinking and smiling. "Sir Harry. Lady Mortimer. I wasn't expecting to see you."

Kat looked at Harry who – with a shrug – seemed at a loss for words. Down the corridor behind him, she could see the faces of inquisitive neighbours beginning to appear, doors opening.

"Hello, Percy," she said. Then she let go of Simone's arms and stepped back. "Why don't we all go inside. And perhaps, Simone, you can explain what's going on here?"

The singer rolled her eyes, then pulled the door open as if it was an annoying obstacle. "Come in. I – *we* – have nothing to hide!"

That proclamation sounding to Kat much too shrill to actually be true.

SIMONE MADE NO effort to offer them places to sit, leaving them standing in the middle of the room as if they had arrived, unwanted, to sell brushes or offer a chance to redeem souls.

Kat took in the small apartment: cramped but cosy, and probably not enough chairs for them all anyway.

She looked at the man who had attacked them: he leaned against a small sink in the corner, rubbing his wrist, his lank hair falling across his face.

His eyes still glowering at her and Harry.

"Perhaps you should introduce us to your friend?" said Kat to Simone, nodding to the man.

SECRETS ON THE COTE D'AZUR

"Grand idea! He clearly forgot to do that in the corridor," said Harry, and Kat caught his eye, restrained a laugh.

"My brother, Paul," said Simone. "He is just a poor fisherman. He doesn't speak much English."

"All right then. Care to explain exactly *why* he attacked us?" said Harry.

Kat waited as Simone spoke in heavily accented French to her brother – a rapid-fire exchange, ending with the young man just shrugging and shaking his head.

"He says that he thought you were someone else," said Simone.

Kat nodded, though – in fact – she was none the wiser. She turned to Percy.

"Percy – perhaps *you* can explain what you're doing here now? We thought you were picking up the cash?"

"I – er – I wanted to come over," said Percy. "Before I went to the bank, you see. Reassure my Simone that, this time, you would *surely* catch the blackmailers." Then his voice lowered as if knowing the next was asking a lot. "And make them *stop*!"

Kat looked at Harry, not at all sure what was going on here.

"Percy, I have to tell you," said Harry, "we heard the man who we know is blackmailing you, on the phone with someone. A probable conspirator."

Harry let that sentence hang there for a moment. "That man is someone you may even know, a certain—"

But he didn't get the next words out as Simone actually hissed the name out: "*Cedric Latimer.*"

"Latimer!" said Paul, unexpectedly from the corner of the little room. "I *kill* him!"

And Kat realised that – just now, out in the corridor – Paul had mistaken Harry for the blackmailer.

She turned back to Simone.

"Hold on a minute. You *know*?" Kat said. "You already know who's blackmailing the man you are supposedly in love with?"

Simone shook her head. Though it was hard for Kat to read the singer's feelings, one element did stand out: Simone looked like they had her trapped.

"*Non*! Not 'supposedly'. I love Percy. It all became so, so—"

Percy stood up – came to Simone and put his arm around her.

"Perhaps, Simone, it's best if I explain. It is rather complicated. These good people trying to help us, deserve to hear it all."

Kat – for one – thought: *I couldn't agree more.*

And Percy – as if bracing himself for the challenge ahead – took a deep breath. Chest inflating like a bellows as he proceeded to make good on his promise.

14.

THE TRUTH OF AN UNLIKELY ROMANCE

"YOU SEE, THIS Latimer chap approached Simone with his 'plan': namely, to blackmail me, with her help. Must have been just a week or so after I arrived here. At that time, we, of course, didn't know each other." He cleared his throat. "And, um, she agreed."

Kat looked at Simone.

"You agreed to that? Blackmail?"

Simone's eyes were lowered, and she gave the smallest of nods – probably feeling that she was being judged. Which was absolutely true.

And which was probably why the singer spoke up.

"Our mother – she is so very frail..." Simone began, nodding to her brother. "She lives in a small fishing village, along the coast. So very poor. She has nothing. And she is so terribly *malade*. The doctors, the hospital – all so expensive. I would not have thought to do such a thing if not for thoughts of *maman*."

That prompted Harry: "We saw you give something to your brother here."

"Yes. When I can, I give Paul money from my singing for my mother, and even my dear sweet Percy has helped."

"How could I not?" Percy said as if such largesse went without question.

Still, Kat was waiting for the tale of how Simone – the associate of the blackmailer – had become the target's lover.

If that was *in fact what had happened.*

"But Simone, despite her mother's terrible need, simply could *not* continue to do it. And I think, also, things had changed."

At that, Simone looked up, straight at Percy. "Quite soon after we met, I realised what a sweet, dear man Percy was. And soon, my feelings grew beyond fondness, into love. I said to Latimer I had to stop, wanted the whole thing to end. But *non* – he has this man—"

"Capo?" said Harry.

"Yes, *Capo*," said Simone, almost spitting out the word. "He is evil. He said if I told Percy, or went to the police, bad things would happen."

Kat nodded, slowly beginning to understand the situation Simone had been in.

And slowly… believing her.

"In the end though," said the singer, "I knew I could do it no longer. The lies. The deceit. So – this morning – I asked Percy to come here, and I told him *everything*."

At this point in the story, Kat realised she had more than a few questions. She led with the one at the very top of her list.

"This morning? Then, why didn't you go to the police?"

"The police? Why, I would be *ruined*!" said Percy. "The board would sack me from my own company. But also, the divorce, the scandal, it would be too much to bear, and so hard on my dear Simone here."

Percy looked at Simone and slowly nodded as he patted the singer's right hand.

Kat found herself wondering if there were any more

remarkable revelations to be had from this unlikely pair. And, despite everything, she felt a fondness for the quirky duo.

And now, truth on the table, it was time – Kat thought – for the tables to be turned, and for them to share a few revelations of their own.

"SIR HARRY AND I have discovered that Latimer has an accomplice, beyond Capo. But we've been able to do something *more*. Something that should bring you some relief."

The watery eyes of the couple before her looked up. Both seeming on the precipice of crying, or kissing, or perhaps doing both at the same time.

"We got into Latimer's hotel room at the Winchester—"

At that, Percy released Simone's hand, and clapped as if his ship had come in.

"You found the money!"

Harry continued. "No. Not the money, I'm afraid. But we did find the film negatives. Whatever Latimer held over your heads is gone. *Disparu*, as the locals might say."

And though Percy's face showed more than a hint of disappointment, he still managed to force a smile, his moustache riding up in an attempt to be happy with this news, his glass half full.

"That… is wonderful. It means we are now – at least – free of the threat of scandal."

But then, facts being what they are, Kat watched him *schlump* back down in his chair.

"Still – all that money, *gone*! So much money. And another payment being demanded for this afternoon, a so-called last payment. But wait – I won't have to pay that, will I?"

At which point, it was Harry's turn to surprise Kat, as she saw her husband put a steadying hand on Percy's shoulder, as if he could imbue the man with strength.

"Been thinking about that, Percy. And – while I haven't discussed this with my wife – I think it's best you *make* that payment."

"What?" Percy and Simone said in unison.

"Then Lady Mortimer and I will concoct a plan to get *all* your money back, you see? And – with the negatives in hand, destroyed, money returned – then I guess we might say we've all had a rather successful holiday on the Côte d'Azur."

Kat could see that Percy looked anything but sure about this. With the evidence gone, he was probably thinking: *Suffer the losses, but don't put any more money into the blackmailer's hands.*

He asked the obvious question: "How will you ever do that?"

Harry turned to Kat, his smile never looking more confident.

"Haven't quite figured that out yet," he said. "But I'm sure when Lady Mortimer and I put our heads together, we'll find a way."

Kat had to add, since she could see the look of doubt on both Simone and Percy's faces: "Trust Sir Harry. When it comes to plans – and when it comes to his word – you can take *that* to the bank."

To which Percy muttered, "And hopefully my money as well."

Kat glanced at Harry. The stakes were high.

"Why don't you tell us the instructions for this afternoon's drop?" said Harry. "And then we can set our little plan in motion."

HARRY LOOKED AT the broad walkway that ran along the Antibes seafront. "Fancy a bit of a stroll before we head back?"

"Well, I am mighty curious about this 'plan' of yours."

He laughed, the morning sun bright, making golden ripples on the sea. He fished out his sunglasses.

Sometimes, he thought, *the Riviera can be a little too bright, especially in the morning.*

"Plan? Oh, I'm afraid I don't have a 'plan' at all. I was rather relying on your extraordinarily wide range of skills and ideas to help us shape one?"

Kat laughed. "I thought so. Well, if we're going to make a plan, we need to define said plan's *objectives*."

Harry stopped. An elderly couple walked by, arm in arm – *over-dressed for the day's heat,* he thought. Prancing along beside them on a leash was the smallest of dogs that, if it didn't move, would resemble a mop head.

He waited till the couple passed, nodding a silent greeting, before continuing.

"Right. Objectives, Very useful things. And they are?"

"Find out who's really running this whole show with Latimer. Then take them both out of the game. And – the tricky one – get Percy's cash back. Agreed?"

"Agreed," said Harry. "Put like that, what could be simpler?"

Kat laughed. "Right."

Harry started walking again, the sunglasses cutting down the glare, giving everything a muted, near-pastel look. Kat, too, followed suit, and took his arm in hers.

He glanced over at another couple chatting together at one

of the promenade cafés, thinking, *How nice it would be just to sit in a café with Kat and while away this absolutely gorgeous day.*

But there was important work to do.

"You first," he said.

"Okay," said Kat. "So, I'm thinking, what's their weak spot? I'll tell you. They're *predictable*."

"You're right," said Harry. "Each pickup – same exact MO. We can use that today when we tail them, yes?"

"Any other weaknesses?"

Harry looked out to the sea for a moment.

"Latimer," said Harry, enjoying the way Kat was playing this. "We know he likes the gaming tables. Has a real taste for them – plays big. Rashly, even."

"I bet he doesn't miss a night."

"Yes. We *also* know – whatever his situation – he likes the ladies."

"That the expression?"

"I believe so," said Harry, laughing. "So, if today's pot of cash is the last, then tonight at the casino is our one chance to get it back, yes?"

"Yes," said Kat.

They walked in silence for a few more minutes, nodding and smiling politely at passers-by. *Just an ordinary married couple enjoying the warm Antibes sea air,* thought Harry. *If only they knew.*

Suddenly, Kat stopped, and turned to him. "Harry... I think maybe I *do* have a plan."

"You do?"

"Think so. It's going to need quite a bit of work. And luck. A lot of luck. And... quite a bit of lying. And perhaps some cheating too."

"Well then. That *all* sounds like good fun."

"Fun – oh yes. But also not without risks."

"Even better."

"We'll need help. You think... maybe your friend Wyndham?"

"Oh, I'm *sure* he'd be game for it. Whatever it is!"

"Not just Wyndham," said Kat. "Think we can track down Roscoe?"

"Bet we can," said Harry, smiling as she spun him round, his arm still in hers.

"Okay then! Love your confidence. We'd better get back to Nice," she said. "We'll need to do some *recces*, call in some favours, and we don't have much time."

And, at that, Harry saw that Kat had really started to run with it.

"*Brilliant*," he said.

"You say that all the time."

"No. This time I mean it. Really – brilliant. The game's afoot, Watson, and—"

"Excuse me," Kat said, stopping for a second and leaning close. "Think *I'll* take the role of Sherlock. How about you be the endearing," *closer still,* "ever-lovable and cuddly, Watson?"

"For a cuddle, well, you know me. I'd do anything."

After a quick kiss, Kat took his arm again and they hurried back to the car.

The game ahead, Harry knew, would be a game of high stakes...

And real danger.

15.

FOLLOW THE MONEY

KAT SAT IN the shadows of the tiny café on the Rue Rossetti –
sunglasses on, newly acquired black beret pulled down – and
peered over the top of her copy of *Le Figaro* at the Liberty Bar
tucked deep into the alleyway opposite.

She'd followed Latimer here an hour ago – at just the same
time that Percy was leaving his valise of cash in a new venue on
the other side of Nice.

So far there had been no sign of Capo – and Harry's
suspicion that the afternoon timing suggested an immediate
handover at the club, seemed to be justified.

The thought of Harry made her glance up the street, up to
the top of the hill in the Old Town, where she knew he was
keeping watch.

She picked up her vin blanc and gently raised the glass to
her husband, before taking a sip and bringing her gaze back to
the dingy, dark little street opposite.

ALL RIGHT FOR SOME, thought Harry up on the top of Castle
Hill, as he watched Kat through a pair of Wyndham's powerful
field glasses.

Hot up here. A chilled glass of beer would go down very nicely right now.

He rubbed his eyes, then put the glasses back to his face. He knew neither of them could afford to make the slightest slip now – the entire plan depended on everything falling into place.

A Robert Burns poem from his schoolboy years seemed apt: *"The best laid schemes o' mice an' men gang aft agley."*

What he and Kat would be attempting was *definitely* a scheme.

After an intense afternoon's work, at the end they'd agreed it *should* work, but both of them had done this enough times to know that even the best plans rarely survived intact – not after real contact with the enemy.

That *enemy*, right now in the dark, smoky backroom of the Liberty Bar – and like Kat and Harry – listening out for the sound of the Gnome Rhône.

Which surely must be here soon.

KAT GLANCED AT her bill – tossed onto the table by a surly waiter who acted as if he wanted this strange woman, nursing her *verre du vin,* off the premises – and dropped some coins in the plate.

Time was running out.

Then – at last – the familiar throaty sound of the motorbike in the distance, approaching. And fast.

She settled lower in her chair, eyes pinned on the Liberty Bar. The Gnome Rhône: loud – louder still – until it was now visible at the far end of the narrow street, getting closer.

Right on cue, the door to the bar flew open – and Latimer stepped out, one hand shading his eyes from the evening sun.

Capo pulled the bike to a screeching halt – then, trademark

cigarette still clamped in the corner of his mouth – Kat watched him reach round, unsling his shoulder bag, and pull out… *a valise.*

Percy's valise, for sure. Loaded with one hundred thousand francs.

He handed the valise to Latimer, who popped it open and checked it quickly. Then, without a word, the blackmailer set off down the little street directly towards Kat.

Quickly raising the newspaper so it almost completely obscured her, Kat watched him reach the corner of Rue Rossetti, the street now busy with evening shoppers.

Latimer stopped and glanced around quickly, as if to check he wasn't being followed, then headed off through the bustling crowd up the hill.

Towards the castle.

Kat waited until Capo had spun his bike and zoomed away, then she stood up, dropped the paper, and headed after Latimer.

Everything – so far – going according to plan.

HARRY KNEELED BY one of the more modest gravestones and arranged a small posy of flowers.

In his borrowed overalls, boots and flat cap, clothes any local worker might wear, he felt confident that he blended in here among the handful of other visitors to the hilltop cemetery.

The grave he had chosen was not one of the extravagant marble sarcophagi, or mini temples that jostled in long lines across the walled garden, the shadows of tall cedars lending the place an almost Egyptian air. No, this grave – the current residence of a certain long-departed Pierre le Blanc, *poor chap* – was no rich man's affair. But it did provide the perfect view of the only entrance to the cemetery – while being helpfully obscured by nearby bushes.

Out of habit, Harry patted his holster underneath the overalls – the revolver secure, and easy to reach should the worst happen.

At least, if something did go wrong, there were few innocent bystanders up here who might get caught in the crossfire. So far, he'd seen but a handful of other *mourners* dotted among the tombs.

He scanned the cemetery again, and saw Latimer suddenly appear at the entrance, peer round as if to get his bearings, then head right towards him!

Harry made what he hoped was a convincing sign of the cross, then raised his clasped hands to his face as if in deep prayer, and pressed closer to the gravestone.

It was his best attempt to disappear.

Would Latimer recognise him anyway? They hadn't met – but Harry knew the blackmailer had been at that first party in Cannes, and could have easily seen him and Kat together.

Out of the corner of his eye, he saw Latimer – now just yards away – striding down the gravel path, bag over his shoulder, not even glancing down as he passed Harry and headed towards the far end of the cemetery.

On an instinct, Harry glanced back at the entrance – just in time to see Kat appear briefly, then slip inside, putting the tall tombs between her and Latimer.

He stood and peered round the grave. Latimer fifty yards away, back to him, still moving. Harry crouched, keeping low, and then hurried to his left, to a parallel pathway, aware that Kat was also on the same path, closing on him.

The two of them now moving as one, both low, bent double.

"I *do* love the outfit," he said as she joined him.

"*Très chic*, don't you think?" said Kat, adjusting her beret. "Where's Latimer now?"

"Far corner of the cemetery. Come on, I found a shortcut just past that temple to Zeus."

He zigzagged past a small chapel, and nearly bumped into a surprised old lady in mourning, one hand resting on a gravestone, black net over her face.

"Bonsoir, madame," said Kat politely, as they ran past at a crouch.

"Bonsoir," said the old lady, her voice stern.

In the distance, Harry could still see Latimer – now standing, bag in hand, talking to someone in the shadows. *But to whom?*

He moved left, with Kat right behind him, using another tomb as cover; that tomb bearing a marble statue, entwined angels, small gaps in the stone perhaps allowing a view through?

He pressed tight against the glossy stone, face close to Kat's.

"Worth the risk?" he said.

"*Always*," said Kat.

They turned together and slowly rose, their eyes just coming level with the statue, Harry now able to see Latimer and the person he was talking to, that person held in an embrace, that person...

A woman.

Smartly dressed, hair pinned back, older than Latimer.

"Good *Lord*!" said Harry.

"So much for *Mr* Big."

"I wonder who it is?"

"Oh – *I* can tell you that."

"You can?" said Harry, turning to look at his wife, surprised.

"Yes," said Kat. "It's Lady Alice Nantwich."

"What? Percy's wife?" said Harry.

"You'd never guess from the way she's behaving," said Kat.

Harry turned to look again at the couple.

To see them kissing deeply.

"Well," said Harry. "*Waddya* know – as you might put it."

And they both dropped down again, and sat together, backs against the marble tomb.

"Suddenly," said Harry, "a lot of things I didn't quite understand are falling into place."

"Same here."

"You know – we could just overpower them and hand them over to the local gendarmerie?"

"We could, but, as Percy said, he'd be ruined."

"You're right. And we might never get all his money back."

"And anyway – don't know about you – I was *so* looking forward to tonight's little show."

"Oh, me too," said Harry. "We definitely can't cancel that."

"Come on then," said Kat. "Curtain up at eight, I believe?"

Taking her hand, and staying low, they crept out of the cemetery, the late afternoon sun sending long shadows across their path, colouring the marble a rich, deep red.

16.

DEALER CHOICE

KAT STEPPED OUT of the cab and, careful with her heels on the wooden boards of the pier, hurried round to the other door as if to help Harry get out of his seat.

But a nearby doorman from the casino rushed over to assist.

"Madame, *please!* Allow me," said the doorman, placing one arm under Harry's and lifting him to his feet, the driver of the cab hurriedly completing the manoeuvre by handing Harry his cane.

"Will your father require any further assistance, madame?" said the doorman.

Kat contemplated Harry – his white hair, round spectacles, stooped back, faded dress suit, drooping moustache and ivory cane clutched in one hand – and tried not to smile.

"What do you think, *Papa*?" she said, smiling so sweetly. "Will you need this nice gentleman's help?"

She saw Harry look up at the crowded steps of the casino, the whole place lit up against the night sky, the sound of music and laughter spilling out across the bay.

Harry's voice almost comical in its hoarse wavering.

"Oh, I believe I can manage, my dear," said Harry, taking her hand. "With your help, bless you, child."

And together, slowly, they made their way to the casino.

The image of the two of them – so sweet.

A dutiful daughter taking her aged father to the tables for a little *fun*.

JUST INSIDE THE main doors, and under the great glass dome, Harry stood as if to catch his breath, and looked around, taking in the layout of the place again – doors, windows, stairs, exits.

Through the crowd, in the corner by the cloakroom, he spied Wyndham leaning against a marble pillar, and he steered Kat towards his new friend – with Kat making it appear *she* was steering *him*.

"I *say*, Harry," said Wyndham, smiling and shaking his head. "Damn fine work with the disguise there. Took me a while to spot you."

"We've got our new friend Roscoe to thank for that," said Kat. "He spent an hour with us at the hotel 'building Harry's character' as he called it."

"That boy's a real find," said Wyndham. "He's already got the table going just as you wanted."

"You've made contact with Latimer?" said Harry.

"Ha – we're old chums already," said Wyndham. "Soon as I let him in on the 'secret' that I was playing a crooked table and, for a price, he could have some of the action – well – let's just say he leapt at the opportunity like a trout taking a fly."

"Great! Where is he now?" said Kat, and Harry saw her look around, checking the crowd.

"Don't worry, he popped out onto the verandah for a breath of fresh air – or rather, to tot up his winnings so far, I'm sure."

"So, everything's going to plan?" said Kat.

"Like clockwork," said Wyndham. "He and I are both a

hundred thousand up, and he keeps bringing more chips to the table."

"Sounds like all of Percy's money's in play?" said Harry.

"With that pile of chips growing? I would think so," said Wyndham. "Anyway, Roscoe's lining up the cards and the wins for us, all as planned, and Latimer's lapping it up. The pit boss… catching nothing, by the way."

Harry looked at Kat. Big grin on his face.

"What do you think?" he said. "Time for my entrance?"

"Sounds like it," said Kat.

"Jolly good," said Wyndham. "Okay. The second I see you approaching, Harry, I shall make my excuses, take my winnings – and leave you a seat at the table. Latimer won't have time to wonder where I've gone – or why. He'll be far too interested in your arrival, sensing – perhaps – a pigeon, all ready to be plucked. And, I must say, I've never seen a more convincing victim!"

"Excellent work, old chap," said Harry, patting Wyndham on the shoulder. "You go ahead now – I'll see you in there."

Then he turned to Kat.

"How do I look?" he said.

He waited while she leaned close and adjusted his jacket over his shoulder holster, then gave him a peck on his wrinkled cheek.

"Oh, Papa," she said, her eyes twinkling. "Please don't lose the family fortune *again*."

"I shall do my very best, my angel," said Harry, his wobbly voice in character.

Then he held her eye and whispered: "See you on the other side, eh?"

"On the other side," said Kat, then she turned and left him

SECRETS ON THE COTE D'AZUR

alone.

He watched her head to the stairs and then up to the balcony, her long turquoise dress so elegant, her jewels sparkling, her clutch bag of woven gold shining under the chandeliers.

Then he tapped his cane on the marble floor – and slowly headed into the gaming room.

KAT STOOD IN the shadows at the very end of the balcony, sipping champagne and looking down on the gaming tables below.

As ever, the room was crowded, bustling, all the tables busy, chips and cards flashing across the velvet, the roulette tables noisy.

Directly opposite, twenty feet below, she could see Roscoe's table, the game – *chemin de fer* – underway, just like the night before, Latimer confident, an enormous heap of chips stacked in front of him.

And, seated facing him, a frail old man, one hand atop a cane, the other reaching out one at a time for the cards as they came from the shoe, aged hands turning the cards slowly as required.

Her husband, playing the role of his life.

She watched as the shoe was handed to Harry and another round of the game commenced. Latimer – so bullish, a little crowd around him (mostly female, she noticed), the blackmailer laughing as he confidently shoved a stack of chips forward.

Kat guessed he was thinking this senile old fellow was clearly a walkover.

The cards slid out of the shoe – Harry now playing just

against Latimer, the rest of the table watching, curious perhaps. The frail hands turned the cards, chips propelled, stacked. Another card turn.

A collective gasp from the table as Kat saw Harry turn over his hand *and win*.

She looked quickly at Latimer — the man confused, eyes narrowed, trying to work out how he got the odds wrong, how this could have happened — as a great stack of his chips was swept up by Roscoe and deposited right in front of the "old man".

A group of onlookers now gathered behind Harry. Some pats of encouragement on his shoulder, laughter, bemusement. Harry shrugging good-naturedly — as if even he didn't understand how he might have won — and the game continued.

And then Harry won again.

Latimer's mountain of chips was now halved, while Harry's had doubled. Thousands of francs in play. Kat could see a sheen of sweat on Latimer's forehead — his little coterie of supporters drifting away, his actions sharper, faster, his cards flipping over angrily.

And then a movement at the far end of the balcony caught Kat's eye, and she saw a figure she recognised approaching.

Lady Nantwich.

The woman's eyes were absolutely fixed on Latimer's table below, getting closer now, clearly wanting to be right above the action.

Kat knew that Lady Nantwich hadn't seen her, standing here in the shadows, and she waited until they were just a few feet apart before saying: "Such an exciting game, *chemin de fer*, wouldn't you agree, Lady Nantwich?"

Kat saw the woman spin round fast.

"Lady Mortimer – how surprising to see *you* here."

Kat stepped forward, out of the shadows.

"Any particular table interest you?" she said, nodding to the crowded room below.

"Oh, I don't know," said Lady Nantwich, "I'm not really an *habituée* of the tables."

"Really?" said Kat. "That surprises me. Since it looks like your accomplice is down there – right now – losing a fortune."

"Accomplice, my dear? I'm sure I don't know what you are talking about."

Kat moved closer, until she was just feet away, then indicated the table below.

"Cedric Latimer," she said. "Half an hour ago he had a couple of hundred thousand francs in play. But now, sadly… *tant pis.* Well, see for yourself."

She waited as Lady Nantwich, almost begrudgingly, moved her eyes from Kat and focused on the game below.

"See that *very* old gentleman down there?" said Kat. "He seems to be having the most extraordinary luck."

"Indeed."

Kat detected a shakiness in Lady Nantwich's single word.

"Yes. In fact, it looks very much to me as though – *quel miracle* – he has won nearly all of Mr Latimer's money."

Silence still from Lady Nantwich.

"Or should I say… *Percy's money?*"

The woman turned and shrugged.

"All right," she said. "You've made your damn point. How much do you want?"

"Oh, I don't want *anything.*"

"Cedric's a fool. You can have his share."

Kat shook her head. Latimer clearly meant nothing to the

126

woman. *Was this just about money?*

"Why did you do it?" she said.

Lady Nantwich looked away. "My dear girl, haven't you worked that out yet?" said Lady Nantwich. "And I heard you were such a clever little thing."

Kat ignored the jibe. *For now.*

"You wanted Percy's fortune," she said. "A divorce. And no scandal."

"*Correct.* My marriage to Percy was over a long time ago. I mean – he is such a dreary little man. And *pickles*? The absolute shame of it. But all those years ago I had no choice. I needed his money to keep my estate afloat – and marriage was the only way to get it."

"So why not just divorce? Why blackmail him too?"

"Ah – that was Cedric's idea. Tad ambitious, you see. Even greedy. And I needed to keep him happy."

"Because he thought he had a future with you?" said Kat.

"*Exactly.* I can't blame him. He was useful, so I led him along. And he is – most of the time – rather fun. Certainly more fun than my husband."

"But not marriage material for Lady Nantwich?" said Kat.

"Good Lord, no. You see, when it comes to marriage and family honour, some of us do have high standards, *Lady Mortimer.*"

Kat smiled. The implied insult from this woman did not dent her one bit. In fact – the opposite – *she would enjoy turning the tables on her when this was all over.*

She heard another cheer go up from the table below, and she looked down into the room. Another win for Harry – the pile in front of him absolutely immense – a crowd now gathered around him.

The game – *once afoot* – now nearly over.
Latimer's chips gone – his head shaking in rage.
The man looking crushed.
But then, in a second, everything changed.

17.

THE END OF THE PIER SHOW

HARRY SENSED THAT Latimer had reached breaking point, and was already bracing himself for the man's reaction, whatever it might be.

But, even so, he was surprised at the suddenness – and the violence.

He saw Latimer kick back his chair and stand – people suddenly scattering on all sides.

"It's rigged!" he shouted. "The damn table's rigged!"

Across the room – Harry sensed the games all come to an abrupt halt. A collective gasp. Slowly, he pushed back his own chair, in readiness for what might come.

Latimer hurled his cards to the floor, then bounded round the table to Harry.

Harry, still in character, feebly rising from his seat: "My *dear* chap, 'tis purely the luck of the cards, a game of chance."

"Luck of the damn cards?" said Latimer, roughly grabbing Harry's lapels, everything happening in seconds. "You scoundrel!"

Another gasp from the crowd. Harry saw Roscoe moving quickly.

"Sir, please! I must ask you to unhand that—"

Harry allowed himself to be lifted up, seeing Latimer's face red, sweat-stained, a vein bulging on his forehead, his eyes bulging.

His scrutiny, now close.

"*Wait a minute,*" said Latimer, peering now intently at Harry's face. "You're *not*—"

Harry felt his lips sting as Latimer ripped his false moustache from his face, and then his wig went tumbling onto the table, white powder billowing.

"What the...? Who the *hell* are you?"

But instead of answering, Harry brought both his arms up fast, explosively, between Latimer's, forcing his grip apart and making the man fall back against the table.

"Afraid it's game over, old chap," he said, stepping back and brushing his jacket down. "Someone always has to lose. *Your turn in the barrel,* as they say. Shame, eh?"

He nodded to the far side of the room where Wyndham was already approaching through the frozen crowd, a gendarme in tow.

For a second, Harry could see Latimer weighing up his options – and then the man reached into his jacket and pulled out a small automatic, pointed it straight at Harry, hand trembling.

Well, well, thought Harry. *Wasn't quite expecting that.*

"No call for guns, Latimer," he said calmly. "That's a game that nobody wins. Don't be a fool. Police already here. Nowhere to go."

He stared at Latimer, the man wide-eyed, thinking: *This could go either way.*

Suddenly, Latimer pointed his gun at the chandelier overhead and fired. And then – in the explosion of shattered glass, the smell of cordite, and the screams of the crowd – Harry saw him run for the exit.

Unbuttoning his jacket, Harry reached in, took out the Webley from his holster, quickly checked the rounds in the chamber, and raced after Latimer through the stunned spectators.

KAT LEANED AGAINST a metal girder in the darkness of the end of the pier, still catching her breath from the race out here. The tang of the sea here so strong, the waves lapping against the struts.

Out across the water she could see all the dazzling reflections from the casino that rose above and behind her.

In the distance, she heard footsteps on the wooden boards, people running, running this way.

"*Il arrive,*" said Paul Sorel, softly. "*Latimer!*"

Kat looked at the young fisherman, standing in the shadows, his eyes bright. As soon as she and Harry had mentioned the plan to him that afternoon, he had leapt at it, Simone translating the requirements, the boy adding his advice.

"You ready?" Kat said.

"Oui!"

This is the revenge he's been waiting for, she thought. Earlier in the evening, just as they were arriving at the casino, Paul had overpowered Capo with the help of a couple of friends, as he waited in Latimer's launch.

Tied up, bound, gagged, the gangster now lay unmoving at Paul's feet, occasionally getting a friendly tap in the stomach from a fisherman's boot if he made the slightest noise.

Latimer's launch was at the end of the pier, moving gently in the slow waters, tethered to a small boarding ladder.

And then Kat heard another gunshot – loud – close by.

She pressed back against the rusty steel girders.

HARRY DUCKED DOWN behind a crate of life preservers as a shot whistled over his head.

Another shot – this time he heard the thud of the round hitting the crate.

Rather appropriately named, he thought.

He poked his head up from cover to see Latimer a hundred yards ahead now, disappearing round the side wall of the casino – the pier here no more than a narrow, boarded walkway.

He looked behind him – Wyndham and the gendarme were even further back, only now realising where the action was.

Gun in hand, Harry edged out of cover and ran, head down, towards the end of the pier.

KAT HEARD THE third shot – that one so close now – and she kicked off her high heels, and took the small automatic from her clutch bag. The magazine already checked, she eased off the safety, breathing slowly, calmly, getting herself ready.

From where she stood, in total darkness, she could see the narrow walkway that skirted the casino. And, as she watched, she saw the flickering movement of a shadow – that shadow getting longer – Latimer's shadow, she knew.

And suddenly, *there was Latimer, moving fast towards her.*

"Capo!" he hissed, getting closer, barely a few feet away now. "Get the damn motor going, you *fool!*"

Kat watched him, still running, look over his shoulder back down the pier: he raised his arm and fired one more shot.

And, in the distance, Kat saw Harry appear at the side of

the building and press himself tight against the wall, no safe way through, while Latimer still had rounds to fire.

"Dammit man!" said Latimer, now at the ladder by the launch, peering down into the darkness below, the boat only half visible. "Where the hell—?"

Now or never, thought Kat.

She stepped slowly across the wooden boards, Latimer still unaware, until she was a yard away.

Then she raised her automatic and pressed it firmly against the back of the blackmailer's head.

Latimer froze.

"Capo's been – well, you see – unavoidably detained," she said. She saw Latimer begin to turn, but she pressed the gun even harder against the man's skull.

"Oh – don't move, Cedric," she said. "And, please, if you would, drop the gun."

After a couple of seconds, Latimer let the gun fall to the wooden boards, and Kat kicked it backwards for Paul to pick up.

"I–I've got more cash, back at my hotel," he said. "We could go halves."

"What is it with you guys?" said Kat. "*Sheesh*! Always *halves*."

"What?"

"No deal, Cedric. Or, at least, not a 'deal' that will benefit you."

Kat heard a police whistle and glanced back down the pier. Harry approaching, smiling now, gun still in hand, and, a way behind him, Wyndham and a group of gendarmes.

"Game's over," she said. "*All of the games.*"

Latimer said nothing for a moment. But then: "Not quite."

And she saw him take a step forward – and *jump* into the

dark sea, twenty feet below.

She peered down into the darkness, and waited until he surfaced, splashing around, clearly not much of a swimmer. Harry joined her, put his arm around her.

"Funny," he said. "All that wonderful planning and we didn't ever dream he'd do *that*."

"Chilly night. I, for one, am certainly not going in after him."

"Bit late for a swim for me as well."

She turned and hugged him tight, then pulled back for a second and kissed him on the lips.

"So, Sir Harry, does the vacation begin now?"

"It most certainly does, *ma cherie*."

And, arm in arm, they headed back down the pier towards the bright lights of the town, as the gendarmes hauled a dripping wet, sombre Latimer from the sea.

18.

RETOUR À PARIS

HARRY PULLED OPEN the double doors of the train's dining car and stepped back to let Kat go first.

The car was crowded, dinner already being served. But he knew they had a cosy table booked at the far end.

The aroma of cooking – so tantalising. Already he was running through that amazing wine list in his head, trying to choose what they would drink tonight.

After the obligatory Pommery, of course.

Had it really only been a week since they were last here on the Train Bleu? Hard to believe. But at least now – after all that hectic, exciting, and even dangerous activity – he and Kat would get some peace and quiet, all to themselves, as the train weaved its way back to Paris.

But then he saw Lavinia! At the window seat of an otherwise empty table for four.

"*Darlings!*" she said, seeing them approach. "*Quelle surprise, non?* I only just managed to get a ticket at the *very* last minute – and, look, my good friend Georges kept a table back for us all. Isn't that simply *wonderful?*"

Harry looked at Kat – she smiled generously.

"How lovely," she said, sliding into the window seat opposite Lavinia, while Harry took the seat next to Kat.

"Er, Aunt Lavinia, we thought you were staying on in

SECRETS ON THE COTE D'AZUR

Cannes for another month?" said Harry.

"Oh, I got so *bored*," said Lavinia. "Nothing ever really happens apart from endless cocktail parties and swimming."

Harry smiled patiently at his aunt.

She leaned closer across the table to them, her voice lower: "Of course — *you two* — well, your fame goes before you. I have absolutely no idea how you managed it, but I hear Lady Nantwich has retreated to deepest Devon in some form of disgrace. Cedric Latimer has disappeared as well! And somehow you tied the knots so nothing leaked to the press!"

"I do know the gendarmes were glad to finally have Capo under lock and key," Kat said.

Lavinia nodded at that.

"And dear, sweet Percy? Apparently, he will now be free to marry that charming young singer."

"Remarkable how these things simply *turn out*, isn't it, Lavinia?" said Harry, with a quick smile to Kat.

"Isn't it?" said Lavinia. Then they all waited as the waiter opened a bottle of Pommery and began to pour. Harry looked up at him.

"Four glasses?" he said.

"Four *indeed*," said Lavinia. "We have another guest who is joining us for dinner. Really the most wonderful, charming new companion I just met — in a compartment right along from my own."

Harry saw Lavinia look over his shoulder to the carriage doors.

"In fact... ah, here he is now. He really is most entertaining. Such a surprise, given his... well... let me introduce you. May I present the Archbishop of New York."

Surprised, Harry turned to the side of the table to see...

White-haired, and dressed in purple clerical robes…

Roscoe Burns.

Looking as surprised as Harry felt.

Harry stood – Kat too.

"Well, it's certainly an honour to meet you, Your Grace," said Harry, trying not to laugh and nodding towards Roscoe's right hand. "I say, does one kiss Your Grace's ring?"

"Um, not necessary," said Roscoe, "when I'm er, off duty, as it were."

"Do sit down, my dear archbishop," said Lavinia, patting the chair opposite Harry. Harry watched the "archbishop" take his seat.

"Such a pleasure to meet you," said Kat, enjoying this as well. "I'm from New York too, you know."

"Really?" said Roscoe.

"Oh yes. And I imagine we must have so many friends in common at St Patrick's."

"Er, indeed."

"And now, how lovely to have you to ourselves for an hour or so," continued Kat. "I can't *wait* to hear your views on whether sinners really can reform. You see – based on recent experience – I do have my doubts."

Harry nearly spluttered into his champagne.

"Redemption. It is, ahem, a *complicated* topic," said Roscoe.

"But, I would think, one that must be so close to your heart?" said Kat, smiling.

"Well, I can see we are going to have *such* an interesting journey back to London," said Lavinia, catching on that something here was *afoot*.

Then she raised her glass. "To new friends!"

"And old," said Kat and Harry together, laughing, as the

train rushed northward in the soft Provençal evening.

NEXT IN THE SERIES:

A DISTANT VOICE

MYDWORTH MYSTERIES #9

Matthew Costello & Neil Richards

It's Midsummer in Mydworth – and celebrated medium Bellamy Smythe is in town with his lucrative supernatural show, claiming he can contact the departed. Still deep in mourning from the loss of her father in the Great War, spinster Alice Wetherby is desperate to make contact with 'The Other Side' and Smythe is happy to oblige – even though Alice is quite broke.

Suspecting that Alice is being played, Harry and Kat investigate. As the Midsummer festivities intensify, they find themselves in a game of high stakes deception and clever tricks, where nothing is what it seems, and everyone is a suspect...

ABOUT THE AUTHORS

Co-authors Neil Richards (based in the UK) and Matthew Costello (based in the US), have been writing together since the mid-90s, creating innovative television, games and best-selling books. Together, they have worked on major projects for the BBC, PBS, Disney Channel, Sony, ABC, Eidos, and Nintendo to name but a few.

Their transatlantic collaboration led to the globally best-selling mystery series, *Cherringham*, which has also been a top-seller as audiobooks read by Neil Dudgeon.

Mydworth Mysteries is their brand new series, set in 1929 Sussex, England, which takes readers back to a world where solving crimes was more difficult — but also sometimes a lot more fun.

Printed in the USA
CPSIA information can be obtained
at www.ICGtesting.com
LVHW051233091123
763265LV00077B/2918

9 781913 331177